The QUEEN of EMERALD FALLS

J. J. DiBenedetto

ISBN: 9781005042561

Any references to historical events, real people, or real places are used factiously. Names, characters and places are products of the author's imagination.

Cover design by: Rachel Rossano (www.rachelrossano.com)
Book design by: Colleen Sheehan (www.ampersandbookinteriors.com)

Printed by: Amazon
First printing: December 2020

Writing Dreams
Arlington, Virginia
www.jjdibenedetto.com

Also from

THE AUTHOR

All books available in paperback, and as Audible audiobooks!

All available at:
www.amazon.com
and
www.jjdibenedetto.com

1.

ARIEL - NOW

Ariel Jones-Hardy stared at the envelope. She'd found it in the old hiding spot on the top shelf in the back corner of the hall closet, the same place her parents – usually her father, being the more organized of the two - always squirreled away her gifts.

It never ceased to amaze her that after twenty-one years, they still had no idea she knew about it, that no birthday or Christmas or graduation gift was ever a surprise to her.

Well, maybe not twenty-one years; really only fifteen or sixteen. She hadn't properly understood about yearly gifts until she was four or so, and then it had been another year before she figured out how to climb up to the top shelf in the back of the closet to see all the goodies there.

Except, maybe, they did know. Really thinking about it now, how could they not have known all along? They were both smart. Her father was a doctor, after all, and more than that, a psychiatrist. And while her mother might not have had her father's education, she had enough low cunning and street smarts for the both of them with plenty to spare. Of course they knew.

It was a manila envelope, and it was thick; Ariel could feel a book inside. Or a notebook? She thought she could feel something round, possibly spiral binding. And on the envelope itself was written simply:

For Ariel — do not open before October 25, 2018.

Which was tomorrow. And also, certainly not coincidentally, her twenty-first birthday.

It was written in her mother's hand, beautiful writing with lots of flourishes on the letters, until she got to "October" at which point it became nearly illegible, almost as if her mother had suddenly been distracted in the middle of writing it. Which was almost certainly what had actually happened. Sheryl Jones was nothing if not easily distracted.

If it had been in her father's writing, Ariel might have obeyed the instruction, put the envelope back in the closet and waited until her birthday proper to read it. But it was her mother who had written it, and her mother never set much store by rules. Mostly she regarded them as guidelines, or suggestions; things she might obey, or not, depending on how she felt at the moment. And in that regard, Ariel was definitely her mother's daughter.

"You owe me a dollar, Sheryl. I said she'd open it up the minute she found it."

Her father's voice broke Ariel's concentration. She'd been so engrossed in the book - the diary, as it had turned out - she hadn't even heard her parents coming up the steps, or their footsteps on the hardwood floor of the hallway.

There was no point pretending she was doing anything other than exactly what it looked like she was doing; she was sitting on the floor, her back up against the wall, the closet door still open, the diary in her hand.

"I'm sorry," she said. "I couldn't help myself, I had to look in the closet, and anyway, I'm only a day early." Not even a day now; from her position on the floor, she could see the window high up near the ceiling, and it was almost totally dark out. How long had she been sitting her reading here mother's diary? It really *had* been engrossing, except that wasn't nearly a strong enough word to describe it.

"It's fine, honey," her mother said, offering a hand to help her up. "I knew you wouldn't resist."

Her father rolled his eyes at her mother; something she'd seen him do about a million times over the years. "Then why did you bet me?"

"Why do you think I only bet a dollar, Doc? Have you ever known me to make a stupid bet?" Even before she finished speaking, her mother was glaring at him. "Never mind, don't answer that."

The diary had been full of risky bets by both her parents, and bets that went so far beyond risky Ariel wasn't sure there was a word for them.

"Is this all true, Mom?" Ariel held up the diary. "Everything you wrote about, it all really happened?" She knew that at least some of it had to be true; she'd heard bits and pieces of some of the stories there before, and not only from her parents. There was too much independent verification for the diary to be simply the product of her mother's imagination.

Before her mother could answer, her father grabbed the book and opened it to the first page, the one dated April 3, 1994 - three years before she'd even been born. He read for a few seconds, then exclaimed, "Ha!" He flipped a page, read some more, and again "Ha!" He picked another page, somewhere near the middle, then another two or three more, each accompanied by another "Ha!"

"Just what is the ha-haing all about, Doc? Every word I wrote in that journal is the God's honest truth! You told me I had to do that, there was no point keeping it if I didn't write the truth."

She was telling the truth now; as flighty as her mother often was, as often as she shaded the truth, if not outright lied, Ariel could always tell when she was being honest.

"Oh, it's the truth, just not the whole truth." Her father put an arm around her mother. "And since Ariel knows this much," he waved the book around, "we may as tell her everything else. Preferably over a good bottle of wine." Now he tuned to her, a glint in his eye. "As a gift to your parents, I trust you can pretend that it'll be your first sip of wine?"

"I think I can manage that, Dad." She grinned up at him. "Especially if it's the 2011 Special Reserve Chardonnay that you've had chilling in the fridge since Saturday."

"Sheryl," her father said, "I think we've created a monster."

"A monster with good taste, Doc. Probably the best we could have hoped for."

The 2011 was opened and drunk, along with a meal consisting of all Ariel's favorites from the rooftop Grand Dining Room at the Cosmopolitan Court hotel. Over dessert, and a bottle of 2007 claret that was even better than the chardonnay, her mother began expanding on the tales related in the diary. "You're going to let me tell it, right, Doc?"

"I will only chime in with corrections or supplementary details." Ariel imagined there were going to be a lot of those.

"Fine, Doc. corrections and details only. So let me set the stage. It was the spring of 1994. Bill Clinton was President, and the governor was...well, it doesn't really matter, he doesn't come into it anyway, I was just creating the mood. Bill Clinton, and *The Lion King*, that was 1994, right, Doc?" Her father shrugged. He did that a lot. "And the Olympics, right? The crazy figure skater, the one who hit the other one with a lead pipe? Tanya Tucker, wasn't that her name?"

Now her father sighed. He did that a lot, too. "Tanya Tucker is a country singer, Sheryl."

"Oh, right," her mother said. "I knew that. 'Stand By Your Man.'" She almost sang the words, producing another sigh from her father.

"Tammy Wynette sang that. Tanya Tucker sang," her father paused for a moment, clearly trying, and failing, to recall a song Tanya Tucker had sung. It was strange to see him come up empty; that almost never happened. "Well, I'm sure she sang a lot of songs, but that's neither here nor there. You were thinking of Tonya Harding, and it was her boyfriend who actually hit the other skater with a lead pipe."

"Whatever. Like I said, I'm just setting the mood. *The Lion King*, and Bill Clinton, and Tonya Harding, and wasn't *Fraiser* on TV? You used to get so annoyed at that show, Doc."

This time her father growled. "Must you mention that miserable program? It made a mockery of my profession! Fraiser Crane was completely unrepresentative of a practicing psychiatrist, and his brother was even worse! It should never have been allowed on the air!"

"Moving on," her mother said breezily, "Spring of 1994. Bill Clinton, *The Lion King*, Tonya Harding, *Fraiser*, and then there we were, me and your father..."

2.

SHERYL – THEN

Sheryl Jones stood in the front hallway of the Chalet, looking into the eyes of its owner. Trying to, anyway; it was difficult to maintain eye contact when the other person was giving you a death stare.

He was overreacting, of course. Yes, they'd had a few arguments. Yes, she'd barged into his office right in the middle of what had turned out to be a very intense session with a patient, but how was she supposed to know that? And, yes, maybe, possibly, the joke she'd played on him for April Fools was not, strictly speaking, in the best taste.

It was still funny.

And if Dr. Jon Hardy could only laugh at himself once in a while like a normal person, he would have thought so too, and they'd be enjoying a romantic dinner right now instead of standing awkwardly in the front hallway, underneath the chandelier that she'd picked out and spent weeks talking him around to buying.

"Doc," she began, but he only glared all the more at her little nickname for him. It wasn't even a nickname, really - he was an actual doctor, after all. "Jon. For the fifth time, I'm sorry about the joke. I didn't mean anything by it."

"Sheryl, your joke brought every teenager and tweenager in the county out here. I was cleaning eggs and rotten fruit out of the gutters until ten o'clock last night."

She knew that. He'd told her, repeatedly. "I said I'm sorry! I mean it!"

The glare changed to something else. Something like sadness, maybe. "I know you mean it, Sheryl. You always mean it. But you never mean it enough to change your behavior. Or even to stop and think about the consequences."

There was no anger, or even annoyance in his voice. Just that sadness, mixed with what sounded like disappointment. But worse than either of those was the note of resignation, possibly even hopelessness. She'd never heard that from him, or at any rate not directed at her.

"That's not fair!" She couldn't help it; the words came out before she could properly consider them. "I mean, maybe you're right. I don't always think things through, and maybe sometimes I go a little overboard. But you know I'd never do anything to purposely hurt you. I..."

"Stop right there." He said it without even disappointment this time, just a stone-faced calm that was the worst thing of all in this whole miserable conversation. "You can't say that. Not now, not when I'm yelling at you. That's not how it works."

That was stupid. No, ridiculous. And yet true all the same.

He was absolutely right. She knew that Jon loved her, and that he knew that she loved him. But neither of them had ever said those three little words to the other, not in the correct order, at the correct moment. And this *wasn't* the time; you didn't use those three words to get out of an argument. Not if you actually *did* love the other person.

"Fair enough." Couldn't he see how much she'd grown, that seven months ago she wouldn't have understood that, and even if she had, she could never have admitted it? "But don't you think we could sit down like civilized people and talk this out?" Sitting next to each other on the beautiful leather love-seat it had taken six visits to the furniture store to badger him into buying, she could fix everything. She could get through to him, make him see that all the arguments didn't really mean anything. That they were obviously right for each other, that nothing could come between them for long.

"No, Sheryl. Not this time. I think it's best if you go."

He was throwing her out! Out of what had almost been her home! "I'm not going, Jon. Not until we sort everything out." There was a hint - more than a hint - of pleading in her voice, and she hadn't even done that on purpose. But it didn't make any difference.

"I don't believe we can, Sheryl. If you go now, before either of us says anything we would regret later, we can still remain civil. Friends, even."

That was possible, of course. She had several exes who she was on civil terms with. More or less. Depending on how generous your definition of "civil" was. But it wouldn't be the case for them. The feelings were too strong, ran too deep, for the two of them to be anything except lovers, or to despise each other with a hate that would make the Grinch's loathing for Christmas look like a passing snit.

She could stay. She could put a hand on his arm, pull him close, hold him tightly as though both their lives depended on it. And if she did, things might move to that loveseat, and to a kiss, and then to more than a kiss, and once that happened, they might not even make it to the bedroom before matters reached their natural conclusion.

Seven months ago, before she'd met Jon, if she'd found herself in this exact situation with any of her exes, that's exactly what she'd have done. Paper over the cracks with a few moments of passion. But that's why they were all exes, wasn't it? And the fact she could recognize that proved Jon was wrong about her, wrong that she didn't think things through.

The only way she could prove it to *him*, though, was to do as he asked, to leave now, and let him replay her words, and her actions, and every emotion that she knew was showing in her eyes right now, until he realized for himself how much she had learned during their time together. And how much he'd learned, too.

"Fine, Doc. I'll go. But before I do, let me say good night to you properly." And she did, with a kiss that she hoped - uncharitable thought though it was - would leave him needing a *very* cold shower.

By the time Sheryl opened the door to her apartment, she needed a cold shower herself, as a distraction if nothing else. She'd been proud of herself for leaving the way she had, with her dignity fully intact, but it had occurred to her on the drive home that she could, in fact, see Jon's home from the bedroom window of her unit on the twenty-third floor of the West Tower of the Emerald Falls Condominiums.

That had been an unwelcome thought. It was a lot harder to retain her dignity when all she had to do was raise the blinds in order to look out at the Chalet and imagine what Jon might be up to. Or, worse, wonder if he was looking out his own bedroom window and staring up at her home in the distance.

The cold shower didn't help. All it did was put her in an even worse mood than she was already in. On top of that, she was sneezing now; could she have made herself ill by standing under the freezing water for ten minutes?

Worst of all, there was no coffee in the house. Or tea. Or hot chocolate. Or even a single, solitary cup-of-soup packet. Nothing even vaguely approaching a hot beverage, anywhere in the place.

That's what she got for not going to the grocery store this afternoon. She'd assumed she could fix things with Jon, and spend the night with him in the Chalet, and enjoy the perfect coffee that came from the $1,400 expresso machine in his kitchen.

Clearly, there wasn't going to be any $1,400 coffee for a while.

In the end, she settled for toast. Which she burned, naturally, but at least it was warm, and a big glob of orange marmalade covered up most of the charred taste. She nibbled on that and checked the answering machine, hoping against hope there was a message from Jon, admitting that he'd overreacted and begging her to come back.

There was a message, but it wasn't from Jon.

"Sheryl, call me back the minute you get this message! It's important!" The voice on the tape belonged to Vanessa Jordan, her partner at Mirage Cosmetics. Her junior partner. Extremely junior. Far too junior to be calling late at night. "We've got a crisis, the ad rep at Vogue Magazine said she's pulling all our ads for next month's issue unless she hears from you right away."

Vanessa was a nervous girl, but having all their ads pulled from Vogue *was* an actual crisis, especially after all the effort she'd put into getting ad space in the magazine, and spending a year's advertising budget on the most gorgeous, eye-catching, unignorable ad possible.

There was nothing for it but to call Vanessa right now. Sheryl retreated to her bedroom and stretched out on the king-size bed. There was no reason not to be comfortable while she dealt with a crisis, after all. She picked up the pink princess telephone on the bedside table and dialed Vanessa's number from memory. The girl picked up on the tenth ring, and she was extremely groggy when she did.

"Who is this?"

"Vanessa, this is your partner. Your senior partner. I am returning your rather frantic call."

"Sheryl?" She felt no guilt at having woken Vanessa up. It *was* a crisis, wasn't it?

"Of course this is Sheryl! You sounded almost hysterical on the message, so tell me what the problem is." Perhaps Vanessa had misunderstood. Maybe there wasn't a problem with Vogue Magazine at all. "And while we're at it, if it is a crisis, why didn't you call my mobile phone? I have it for a reason, you know."

"I did," Vanessa answered. She didn't quite shout, but it was close enough to annoy Sheryl. Junior partners did not yell at senior ones. "But you didn't pick up. Did you forget to charge it again?"

Of course she didn't forget. Did she?

It wasn't impossible. She did occasionally forget to plug the thing in when the battery ran low, which it did with distressing frequency. "We could point fingers all night, but that wouldn't be very productive, would it? No. So tell me about the crisis."

Vanessa did, and if the girl wasn't exaggerating, they really did have a crisis on their hands. There actually was a problem with Vogue. It seemed that the ad rep from the magazine had been contacted - they didn't say by whom - and told in no uncertain terms that if they continued to sell ad space to Mirage Cosmetics, the CEO of Starwood Industries would be displeased, and he might well pull all the ads that his company - and all its divisions and subsidiaries - ran in the magazine, as well as all its sister publications.

Sheryl had a very good idea who that anonymous contact was. "Maribeth Peale! That sneaky, conniving, duplicitous, cheating little…" Sheryl struggled to think of a word awful enough to describe the woman, but even the vilest curses she knew seemed inadequate to the task.

"I know you and Maribeth don't exactly see eye-to-eye," Vanessa said, in what Sheryl took to be an effort to calm her down. This was the wrong night for that.

"Eye-to-eye! Exactly! I'm going to get dressed and march myself on over to her house right now, and look her in her beady, dishonest, soulless eyes and tell her precisely what I think of her!"

"Sheryl, it's ten-thirty at night! She'll call the police on you." She probably would at that. It might still be worth it, except then they'd arrest her, and who would she call to bail her out? Vanessa wouldn't be able to afford it, Jon might still be too annoyed with her to help, and who else was there?

"Well, I did just shower, and I am in my pajamas, I suppose Maribeth can keep until tomorrow. But I can call the Vogue rep."

"Sheryl, it's still ten-thirty at night! If Caitlin," obviously that was the name of the ad rep, "isn't asleep then she's out at a nightclub or on a date or something, and either way she won't appreciate you bothering her. How about you call when you get to the office in the morning, like a sane, civilized person?"

Sheryl let the implication that she was not sane or civilized pass, which as far as she was concerned was definitive proof - not that she needed it! - that she *was* sane and civilized, no matter what anybody else might suggest. Or imply. Or say outright.

"Yes. Let's do it in the morning. I'm sure I can sort all this out in the bright light of day."

She let Vanessa go, presumably to fall right back asleep. But she herself was wide awake, adrenaline coursing through her veins, and nothing to do with it.

Well, there was one thing. There was the Christmas gift Jon had given her. The small one, the little book he'd given her so she could "write down what you're thinking and feeling, see everything on paper so you can process it better." She hadn't looked at the journal in four months, but why not now? She certainly had a lot of thoughts and feelings to write down.

3.

JON - THEN

After Sheryl left, Jon stood there in the front hall and stared at the door for a good ten minutes.

He didn't really expect her to come back. Not tonight, at any rate. He also didn't know how he would feel if she did.

That was troubling. Or possibly even upsetting. Dr. Jon Hardy prided himself on being aware of, and, more importantly, in full control of his feelings at all times. But ever since Sheryl Jones had come into his life - or perhaps crashed into it was a more accurate description - seven months ago, the idea of control had become an illusion. Nothing was under control when Sheryl was around, or even, increasingly, when she wasn't.

Jon had always scoffed at the oft-repeated joke that psychiatrists were the very people most in need of psychiatric help, but, not for the first time in recent months, he wondered if there wasn't some truth to it after all.

If not actual counseling, he could certainly use someone to talk to about Sheryl, about his ever-more-conflicted feelings regarding her, about the way he was starting to question his own decisions.

"This is ridiculous. Why am I standing here like a housepet waiting for his master to come home?" Jon didn't want to know why that particular image had bubbled up from his subconscious. He shook his head and headed to the kitchen, and as he went he couldn't help but notice every item of furniture that Sheryl had harassed him into picking out, every knickknack she'd given him. And there, on the glass coffee table - the one thing he'd held absolutely firm on, even though Sheryl hated it – was the book she'd given him for Christmas. A first edition, in the original German, of Freud's *The Interpretation of Dreams*.

The gift had blown him away, and that, right there, was the paradox of Sheryl Jones. He hadn't asked for the book, or ever even mentioned it. She'd figured it out on her own, and then she'd tracked down a first edition. God only knew how she managed that, because he'd never been able to find it for himself. And while he hadn't had the heart to get it appraised, he knew it had to have cost her well into the four figures. When she put her mind to it, Sheryl could be insightful, thoughtful, passionate and unbelievably generous, more so than anyone else he'd ever met, let alone dated.

She might be gone, but she was still everywhere, in every room of the Chalet. The place itself was a reminder of her;

she'd been the one to recommend it to him when he'd grown tired of that wretched temporary apartment near the university.

The kitchen provided no relief from thoughts of her. The marble island brought back memories of Sheryl's disastrous attempt to make French toast. A glance at the espresso machine called to mind the night she'd somehow caused it to spew hot coffee all over the floor. He still didn't know how she'd managed that; according to the manufacturer, it was physically impossible for the machine to do what she'd made it do.

She'd made over his living room against his will, defiled his kitchen, done unspeakable things to the finest espresso machine money could buy, driven him to distraction in more ways than he could count - and yet, if she were to come walking back through his front door, Jon knew he'd most likely forget all that and kiss her as though both their lives depended on it.

He could call her. It would be the easiest thing in the world. And didn't he tell his patients that most of the obstacles they complained about were of their own making, that they had the power to overcome them, that - usually, anyway - all they really had to do was get out of their own way?

He did. And it was absolutely true. It was also - as so many of those patients remarked at the end of sessions - far easier to tell someone else to do, than to do it oneself.

He went upstairs, hoping a shower would clear his mind, but it didn't help, especially because Sheryl had left a toothbrush, and her fancy $8 a tube imported toothpaste, on the sink. TV didn't help, either. The local news was boring, he didn't care about professional sports and, considering that his office was located in Emerald Falls General Hospital, *ER* was not particularly relaxing viewing.

There was only one thing left to do, but when he finally called Sheryl, he got a busy signal.

It had taken Jon until almost one o'clock in the morning to fall asleep, and it had not been restful once he did. He'd awakened with the remnants of a dream just on the edge of memory - raised voices, slammed doors and shattered windows. It didn't take a psychiatrist to figure out what – and whom - the dream had been about.

A good strong cup of coffee would probably have dispelled those lingering memories, but it was not to be. The espresso machine wasn't working, and this after he'd paid the man from the factory $500 to fix it. He couldn't even blame Sheryl for it this time; she hadn't touched the machine in weeks.

That would have to be a problem for later. He had patients lined up starting at eight-thirty, and if there was nothing else in his life that he could control at the moment, he could at least be on time and do his professional best to help them.

There were a few stray clouds and a refreshingly crisp chill in the air, so he decided to walk to work. It was about two and a half miles to the hospital, but perhaps the walk and the fresh air would clear his head.

It did, too, until he got within sight of the firehouse, only a few blocks down Galley Street from the hospital.

"Why don't you watch where you're going?"

He'd been lost in thought, and he hadn't even noticed that he'd nearly walked right into someone. The someone was blonde, and short - a good four inches shorter than Sheryl - and she wore a Chanel skirt-suit in light pink. Sheryl had a suit that looked almost exactly the same; she said the color was "coral" and she'd mocked him for not knowing the difference between that and pink.

"I'm sorry," Maribeth," he said. It *had* been his fault, he supposed. And, unlike Sheryl, he had no particular feelings one way or the other for Maribeth Peale.

"Oh, Dr. Hardy. I didn't realize it was you." The frown on her face - almost a sneer, really - softened as she looked him up and down.

"It's Jon, please," he said. Sheryl wouldn't approve of that. Maribeth was her mortal enemy. One of them, anyway. At last count, she had three. "Off to work?"

Now the frown was entirely gone, replaced with something close to a smile. "Board meeting. Hospital board, I mean."

He remembered that from his interview. Emerald Falls General was not a huge hospital, and all new physicians who were being considered for full-time appointments had to pass muster with the board. Maribeth hadn't quite flirted with him, and she hadn't exactly hinted that a date with her might go a long way towards expediting the hiring process, but she'd come close to doing both.

He hadn't taken her bait. Not that she was unattractive; she was very pretty, in a severe sort of way. And he had been single at the time. But as a matter of pride, he'd chosen to rely purely on his merits and, obviously, those had carried the day.

Somewhat to his surprise, Maribeth hadn't had any ill-will towards him afterwards, and even after he'd started dating Sheryl, she'd always been civil to him.

"Anything I should know about?"

She shook her head. Not a single hair on her head moved when she did. It was uncanny; how much hairspray did the woman use? "Just routine business. Besides, from what I hear, you've got nothing to worry about. Professionally, anyway."

The phrase "the cat who ate the canary" could be illustrated with the expression on Maribeth's face now. Jon knew he was expected to ask what, precisely, she meant, and he dutifully played his role.

"I'm sure there's something you're itching to tell me, and it doesn't take a doctorate to guess that it involves my friend Ms. Jones."

"Let's just say that you may want to clear your schedule, because your dear friend Ms. Jones is probably going to be needing intensive therapy once she checks in at her office this morning. Some serious anger management wouldn't hurt, either."

For seven months, he'd done his best to keep out of the feud - what an inadequate word! - between Sheryl and Maribeth, and he wasn't about to throw any fuel on the fire by telling the woman that he and Sheryl had fought last night, and his office was probably the last place she'd come regardless of how upset she was by whatever Maribeth had done.

"You know, Maribeth, you and Sheryl are both smart, accomplished, attractive women with a lot to offer the world. Can't you two find something more productive to do than undermine each other at every opportunity?"

She laughed, and it was as genuine a laugh as he'd ever heard from Maribeth Peale. "For a psychiatrist, you don't understand human nature very well, Jon."

"Or perhaps I'm just an inveterate optimist." He continued chatting with her for another block, until he reached the Firehouse Grille. "This is my stop. I can't in good conscience recommend much on the menu, but they do make a surprisingly good cup of coffee." That wasn't fair; their breakfasts were actually quite good, but unfortunately they were also loaded up with enough cholesterol to block a dozen arteries, and he had no desire to be lectured by Dr. Tabitha Starwood at his annual physical next week.

Maribeth went on her way, he got his coffee to go, and as he sipped it walking the last two blocks to the hospital, he wondered if, assuming that whatever Maribeth had done really was as unpleasant as she'd implied, Sheryl might come to see him despite their argument - or breakup, maybe? - last night.

She wasn't in his waiting room, and she'd left no messages with his receptionist, Monique. But when he unlocked the door to his office, there she was, reclining on the couch and staring impatiently up at him. "Monique said you're usually here by eight o'clock. You're late!"

4.

ARIEL - NOW

"I never broke into your office like that, Jon!"

Ariel was impressed that her mother had listened quietly to her father's version of events as long as she had.

"Sheryl, it took me four years to get you to stop doing it! And, by the way, you never did tell me how you always managed to get into my office when Monique wouldn't let you in."

Ariel was curious about that, too. Her mother didn't quite blush, but it was as close as she could manage to it. "You know before I met you, I dated Bob McConnell for a little while."

Now it was Ariel's turn to be surprised. "Dr. Bob? My doctor when I was in grade school? You dated him, Mom?"

Apparently so. "I remember, Sheryl. I remember you dated him for a little while back in 1999, too." Ariel had no memory of that, but it was hardly surprising; she'd been only two years old at the time.

"Well, be that as it may, the point is that we were dating back in - oh, 1991? 1992? Whenever the Robin Hood movie with Kevin Costner came out. Do you know, he got so angry when I made a harmless joke about how good he would look in leggings, especially if he had muscles like Kevin Costner did? He had no sense of humor at all."

Dr. Bob had had a great sense of humor; he was always able to make Ariel laugh during her check-ups. "What did Dr. Bob have to do with you breaking into Dad's office, Mom?"

"Well," she began, her not-quite-blush going a bit redder, "Bob was a safety officer - Jon, you know how every wing of the hospital has one, right?" Her mother didn't wait for her father to answer. "Anyway, he was a safety officer for his wing, and all the safety officers carried a master key that opened all the offices in the hospital - just in case, you know?" Her father nodded. Ariel guessed that he knew what was coming next as surely as she did, and her mother didn't disappoint. "Well, I may have borrowed it off his keyring one night when he was asleep and gotten it copied and put it back before he woke up."

"Mom!" Ariel couldn't help reacting, even though she'd expected that answer. She couldn't say for sure whether she was impressed or appalled by her mother's deviousness.

"I only ever went into your father's office! And possibly the records room once. Or twice. It was so long ago, who can remember ridiculous little details like that?"

Her father wasn't angry, or even annoyed, really. He was trying very hard not to laugh. "You see, Ariel? This is what I meant by the truth but not the whole truth."

Her mother glowered at her and her father in turn. "If you're both finished criticizing me, may I continue the story?"

5.

SHERYL – THEN

"What are you doing in my office?"

Jon looked more surprised than angry, which Sheryl took to be a good sign. "I need moral support, and I know what you said last night, but this is a crisis, and I had nobody else to turn to." She really didn't. Vanessa couldn't be relied upon in a crisis; if she could be trusted when the chips were down, she'd already have solved the problem with Caitlin the ad rep

"Moral support?" He wasn't yelling, and there wasn't that horrible note of disappointment in his voice. That was an encouraging sign.

"And physical support. I need a partner. A wingman. Someone to watch my back while I go into the lion's den." It galled her to admit it, but some truths had to be faced head-on. Going down to Manhattan and confronting the forces of Vogue Magazine on their home turf by herself was a fool's errand.

Jon was smiling now. "You didn't mix that metaphor so much as puree it, Sheryl."

"What are you, the grammar police?" She held her voice below a shout, but she wasn't sure how she managed it. "This is life or death! My company's survival depends on what happens today, and you're here cracking jokes about my metaphors!"

Why was he smiling? What was going on in that oversized brain of his? He'd been surprised when he came in and found her on his couch, but that should have faded by now. And, honestly, he didn't seem as surprised as she'd imagined he might be.

"I'm sure it's not that serious." He wasn't quite laughing at her now, but he wasn't far from it. He knew what was going on - but how?

"Yes it is! It's even worse than that, Doc! And - and – and you already know, don't you? How? How do you know what that horrible woman did?"

He sat down in his big, overstuffed desk chair. "I don't know what she did, but I ran into that 'horrible woman' on my way to the hospital, and she was happy to tell me how pleased she was with herself for - well, for whatever it is that's got you so agitated."

"I am not agitated!"

But she had, without even realizing she'd done so, gotten up from the couch, jumped up on the little coffee table in front of it, and balled her hands into fists. Jon was just staring at her, smiling that same smile, clearly trying not to laugh out loud at her. "I am not agitated, Doctor Hardy," she said, forcing her voice down. "I may be annoyed. Possibly even peeved. But definitely not agitated. None of that matters right now, though. I just need to know whether or not you're going to help me."

He made her plead for it, but in the end, Jon agreed to accompany her down to Manhattan. Of course, he was being persnickety about how they got there; he insisted on driving, because, he'd said, "while you have many fine qualities, your skill behind the wheel is not one of them. Nor is your patience with your fellow citizens who are sharing the road with you."

He also refused to drive all the way down to the city. "The last time I drove into Manhattan, I got three parking tickets in one day. I have no desire to repeat that." So he drove them down to Poughkeepsie, parked at the Metro North station, and then they spent nearly two hours on the train to Grand Central Station.

It was as awkward a two hours as Sheryl could remember spending. For the first hour, they barely spoke at all, despite her best efforts. Or, maybe, she supposed, because of them. It wasn't until the train pulled out of the Tarrytown station, just after eleven o'clock, that they really started communicating. "Tell me honestly," he'd said, "and I mean honestly, because I know you're capable when you set your mind to it, what is the problem between you and Maribeth?"

She bit back the first three or four responses; they were all too snarky, and, she had to admit, too easy. She'd talked him into cancelling an entire day's schedule to help her out, the least she owed him was as honest answer as she could manage. "She thinks she's the queen, you know?" He didn't. "She walks around with her nose in the air, looking down on everybody - well, mostly me, but kind of everybody, really. As if she doesn't poop in the toilet like the rest of us just because she went to some fancy boarding school in Europe and Will Starwood gave her a six carat engagement ring."

"Aren't you exaggerating a little, Sheryl?"

"No! Honestly, it's probably closer to six and a half carats. And that's just the main stone. If you count all the accents around it, it's probably more like eight all together. And what business does anybody have walking around with eight carats worth of flawless, perfectly colorless diamonds on their finger?"

"So it's just jealousy, then?"

"No! Who would even want something so ostentatious on their finger anyway?" She stopped herself; she was trying her best to be honest, wasn't she? "Well, I would, of course, and so would anybody else with an ounce of sense. And yes, I'm jealous, but it's more than that. I don't like being looked down on, just because I didn't go to some ridiculous boarding school and I can't trace my ancestry back twenty generations. Who even cares about that, anyway?" Again, she stopped herself. She had to admit that she cared about it, cared a great deal.

Not that she would trade her own upbringing or her family for anything. "Obviously people care, and it drives me crazy."

Now he nearly smiled. "Let's leave the diagnoses to the professionals, shall we? But I do think we're getting somewhere. It upsets you that other people admire her for all that? For things she had no control over, that she didn't earn?"

"Yes!"

"None of us have any control over the circumstances into which we were born. But what's more important, none of us have any control over what anyone else thinks about those circumstances."

"Maybe," she said. And maybe that got right to the deepest truth of all. "But I can control how people see me now. And so can she, and she goes around like the queen, and I do not for the life of me understand how nobody sees through her!"

"You said that already."

"Well, it's true! And if anybody is going to be the queen of Emerald Falls, it ought to be me! I came to town with nothing but five hundred dollars and a couple of suitcases, and I built my own company," which was absolutely true. "I was married to Brad Starwood." It had only been for six weeks, but it still counted. "I was even on the board of Starwood Industries for a while," if you considered six days to be "a while," anyway. "And I ran the whole hospital fundraiser last year! Nobody else can say all that!"

Jon patted her arm. She'd have preferred an arm around her shoulders, or a full, proper hug, but it was better than nothing. "You are a remarkable woman, Sheryl. I told Maribeth as much this morning."

Sheryl wanted to shout at him, and she didn't even know what she wanted to shout. But she managed to hold it in, taking a deep breath and settling for, "What exactly did you say to her?" in something approaching a calm voice.

He sighed. "I told her that you and she were both smart, accomplished, attractive women with plenty to offer, and why can't the both of you find something better to do than attack each other?"

"What did she say to that?"

"She said I don't understand human nature very well."

Sheryl laughed then, really laughed, for the first time since - well, at least a couple of days. "I guess she and I agree on one thing at least, then."

They went back to small talk after that, but when they finally got off the train, and she was hustling him past the alluring smells of the food hall and towards the exit out to Lexington Ave. and a taxi, he said, "I do have to say, with no disrespect to you, if anybody is the queen of Emerald Falls, it isn't you. Or Maribeth."

She didn't wait for him to finish. She knew who he was going to name, and she couldn't really disagree. "I know. You were about to say Annalise Starwood. Yeah. I can't argue with that."

Maribeth Peale infuriated her. Krista Walker annoyed her to no end, especially when she made eyes at Jon, which she had absolutely no right to do, ever. Isaac Carter had a smarmy way about him that made her want to take a shower whenever she was forced to be in the same room as him. But Annalise Starwood terrified her; the woman could cut your throat and leave you thinking you'd asked her to do it as a favor. "You know, as long as I'm being honest, I have to admit she scares the hell out of me."

"Me, too," Jon said, and this time, finally, just as they emerged into the early spring chill, he put his arm around her.

6.

JON - THEN

Jon didn't particularly like Manhattan. It was too crowded, too noisy, too - too everything. This trip was no exception. The Metro North train had been crowded, Grand Central Station had been a zoo and the taxi driver had done his level best to try and kill them. Those all seemed like bad omens.

Not that he believed in omens, of course. At any rate, he hadn't believed in them before he'd met Sheryl. After seven months of knowing her, though, he was seeing them all over the place.

"Come on, Doc. We want to catch her right after she's back from lunch. Vanessa said she usually eats early and she's back at her desk by twelve-thirty. And you ought to know, a full tummy makes for an easier negotiation, right?"

If the stereotypes were anything to go by, someone who worked for a magazine like Vogue - even in the back office - didn't seem likely to ever have a full tummy. But there seemed little point mentioning that. "We can hope, Sheryl." He also hoped that she had some idea where to find the woman they'd travelled nearly three hours to see. He'd had no idea the magazine was headquartered in a massive skyscraper, although he probably should have assumed it. "Do you happen to know where in this monstrous edifice she works, by the way?"

She glared at him. He glared right back. "You think I would come all this way and not be prepared?" He continued glaring; there was no need to point out any of the occasions when she'd gone off half cocked, or, more often, not-at-all cocked. "Fine. She's on the 49th floor, in the consolidated sales office, on the south side of the building."

The 49th floor would be over five hundred feet up; Jon was not acrophobic, but that *was* awfully high.

As it turned out they had to go even higher than that. Once they passed through security, and it was verified that Sheryl actually did have an appointment, the guard directed them to an express elevator that zoomed them up to the sky lobby on the 64th floor, from which they caught a local elevator back down to the 49th.

"When did you manage to get an appointment?"

"In the taxi. While you were too busy closing your eyes in terror - which isn't very manly, by the way - I was on the phone with Vanessa, and she earned her salary for today by arranging things with Caitlin."

The 49th floor was a maze; not at all what Jon imagined the offices of a fashion magazine would look like. He had pictured an open, airy space that would foster creativity, but instead it was a rabbit warren of cubicles, none of them decorated or personalized in any way, interspersed with tiny offices. The closet in his own office at the hospital was bigger than most of them. And for the most part, they didn't even have any windows.

Caitlin Frobisher's office was one of those; it might be eighty square feet; there were prison cells that were bigger. When they entered - the door was open - Jon noted that all of two of the walls were taken up with bookshelves housing dozens of binders, and the third wall had a huge planning calendar pinned up, with a box for each day of the year, and every box filled with tiny but fanatically neat writing.

"You must be Ms. Jones," the woman said, not standing up to greet them. "And..."

"Dr. Hardy," Jon said. "I'm Ms. Jones'..." He wasn't sure exactly how to describe himself in a way that wouldn't sound ridiculous, but Sheryl had an answer ready to go.

"He's an executive consultant. Customer research, branding, psychographics, you understand how important that is in our business, I'm sure."

Psychographics? Jon had never heard the word before, but Caitlin nodded at it, so Sheryl must not have simply made it up on the spot.

"Of course," Caitlin said. She had yet to smile, or do anything that suggested welcoming or warmth or any positive human emotion. It wasn't surprising; how could you have any positive emotions working in a tiny, windowless closet like this? She must have been paid well, though; Jon had seen the jacket Caitlin was wearing in a catalog Sheryl had on her coffee table a few weeks ago, and if his memory served, it cost $5,500. "But I don't see how any of that pertains to your advertising account. As I'm sure Ms. Jordan explained to you, we simply cannot do business with Mirage Cosmetics. It represents a conflict of interest for the magazine."

"What's the conflict?" Sheryl was doing her best to keep her tone calm and controlled, but Jon could hear hysteria starting to creep in.

"As I'm sure you understand," Caitlin said, in a flat, emotionless voice, "that's not something I am at liberty to discuss."

Sheryl was close to a full-on eruption, but she managed to answer without shouting, barely. "It's Starwood Industries. I don't know what Noah Starwood said to you, or your boss, or whoever, but whatever it was, it's not true, I can guarantee you that." Sheryl hadn't mentioned the name of the Starwood patriarch back in his office or on the trip down – mostly she'd ranted about Maribeth Peale – but it made sense that the chief stockholder and President of the family business would be the one to dictate terms, when dictating terms was required.

Caitlin definitely reacted to the mention of Starwood Industries. It wasn't much of a reaction, but Jon saw the slight narrowing of her eyes, the tiny, almost inaudible sigh. Sheryl did too, and she pounced. "I knew it! Tell me what that miserable old goat said!" She was leaning over the desk, her face only inches from Caitlin's. "Never mind, it doesn't matter. He probably threatened to pull all his ads, but that's fine. Whatever business you lose from him, I'll make it up double. Write up a contract and I'll sign right now."

Jon was certain she would, no matter that such a thing was madness, or that she'd never be able to honor a contract like that without bankrupting her company.

"Ms. Jones," Jon said, pulling her back from the ad rep, who now, finally, was looking a bit alarmed. "Perhaps we don't need to be quite so rash. I am sure there is some other way we can work this out to everyone's advantage."

He could feel Sheryl's pent-up energy. It took all his strength to hold her back. But his words seemed to register with her. "I'm sure there is," she said through gritted teeth.

Caitlin wasn't convinced. Now that he was restraining Sheryl, her bored expression had returned. "I don't see what there is to work out. And I do have real business to attend to."

Jon took a deep breath; the woman was getting on his nerves as surely as she was on Sheryl's. But nothing would be served by losing his temper. "Well, Ms. Jones would very much like her ads to run as scheduled, and I think that if we all put our minds to it, we can find a way to run them without upsetting Noah Starwood."

"I don't think so," Caitlin said, in a voice that was now close to robotic.

"Well, I do." Jon said, mentally cursing himself for agreeing to come on this trip at all. But he had, he was here, and he could see one thing that might produce a change of heart in the icy Ms. Frobisher. "You know, and I say this purely as an aside, Ms. Jones happens to have an exquisite Hermès scarf that she bought in Barcelona last Christmas, and it would complement your coat just perfectly. It's cerulean blue, and the pattern - well, it would be so striking on you. But as I'm sure you're aware, they're produced in such limited quantities, I can't imagine where you could ever find one precisely like it. And that's such a shame."

Sheryl turned and glared up at him. He had actually bought it for her on that trip to Spain, and it was the first serious gift he had bought her. But it would be sacrificed for – well, perhaps not a noble cause, but definitely one dear to her heart.

For her part, Caitlin was a little more interested in the conversation now. "You'll have to tell me exactly where you bought it."

"I doubt they'd have another one like it," Sheryl said, making what appeared to be a superhuman effort to speak calmly. "But you know what, it really would look much better on you than it does on me. Maybe I'll Fedex it down to you as soon as I get back to Emerald Falls."

"That's quite generous," Caitlin said, keeping an admirably straight face. "If you really did do something that kind, purely out of the goodness of your heart, and with no expectation of anything in return, I suppose I might be moved to do something generous as well."

Greed was one of the primal motivators of human behavior; it rarely failed. "I don't think anything like that would really be necessary," Jon said. "I'm sure Ms. Jones wouldn't expect anything in return. But it does occur to me that pulling all the Mirage Cosmetics ads from next month's issue is a lot of effort, and I imagine that you work with very strict deadlines. I wouldn't be surprised if it were too late to pull the ads without causing a lot of unnecessary difficulty and expense for the magazine." He grinned now. "But I don't work in the publishing field, of course. You're the expert, I'm sure you would know best."

7.

ARIEL – NOW

"I still say you gave away the scarf just to spite me, because you were mad from our argument." Ariel wasn't surprised; her mother had gone on in the diary for three full pages about it. Her mother could hold a grudge like nobody else.

"If I was spiting anyone, it was myself. I spent five hours searching all over Barcelona for the perfect first Christmas gift for you. Remember the next-to-last day before we flew home, when I told you I was going down to the spa because I needed to decompress after all the ridiculous things that happened in Mallorca?" Ariel had heard the story of what happened on her parents' first-ever vacation together, when they got mixed up with a crazy American student, her clueless brother and a Russian spy. She wouldn't have believed a word of it, except, well, it was completely believable that her mother would get caught up in something so absurd, and, besides, there were pictures.

"You never told me that!" Her mother was staring at her father in disbelief, her wineglass in danger of tipping over and spilling some really outstanding port onto the table.

"Of course I never told you," her father said. "That's not the sort of thing a gentleman ought to tell." He turned to Ariel. "And let that be a lesson to you, young lady. No man worth your attention will ever brag about the lengths he goes to, to please you. He simply does it, and he is grateful for the opportunity to show you how much he treasures you."

That was good advice; of course, she'd heard variations on that lesson from both her parents starting from her first day in middle school.

"Your father is right, Ariel. A lady should always be treasured." She focused back on Jon. "You really do treasure me, don't you?"

Ariel expected him to have a snappy comeback, but there was none; he just looked back at her mother, with nothing but love and sincerity in his eyes. "Always. From the moment we first met." And that's when her mother set down her glass, ran over to her father, and kissed him. And went on kissing him, clearly unaware of how uncomfortable it was for Ariel to watch.

It went on for what seemed like hours, but was probably only twenty or thirty seconds. When they were done, and her mother sat back down, her father smiled and said, "I hope you believe me now. It was never spite. Only an honest desire to keep you from starting a war with Noah Starwood, or running Mirage into the ground."

Obviously he'd succeeded. Ariel had been to the Starwood mansion on a few occasions before old Noah had died a few years ago. She'd only been a child, of course, and not at all interested in the business dealings that the adults mostly talked about, but it had always seemed to her that Noah Starwood had a soft spot for her mother. And equally obviously, Mirage Cosmetics was still in business, still making money.

"I guess it's a good thing you had Dad looking out for you, Mom."

Her father laughed. "You don't know the half of it, Ariel. Believe me. But we'll get to that."'

8.

SHERYL - THEN

She knew she shouldn't have done it. She knew what Jon would say - heck, what any rational person would say. But she did it anyway. How could she not?

The morning that the June issue of Vogue Magazine hit the newsstands, Sheryl went down to Bailey's Books and News over on Third St and bought every copy they had. Once she did that, she headed directly to the Starwood Industries building, and straight up to the 14th floor office of Maribeth Peale. She wasn't sure what time the woman rose from her crypt, but if Maribeth was not there yet, so much the better. In that case, she could leave a copy of the magazine on her desk, opened to the glorious two-page Mirage Cosmetics ad on pages 82-83.

"Who let you in the building? I thought we had security." Maribeth was at work, obviously. And she was wearing that same Chanel suit that she'd obviously only bought in imitation of the one in Sheryl's own closet. How pathetic did you have to be to do that?

"I'm always welcome here. I am a former board member of Starwood Industries. And a former Mrs. Starwood. Neither of which you've managed yet, Maribeth."

Maribeth held up her left hand, making sure the ostentatiously large diamond on her ring finger caught the sunlight. "Patience, Sheryl. All in good time. Anything worth doing is worth doing right, and I have no intention of being a former Mrs. Starwood once I'm officially part of the family. Once I'm in, I don't ever plan on going away."

"Like toxic mold," Sheryl answered, then gave her best fake-embarrassed laugh. "Oh, did I say that out loud?"

Maribeth didn't rise to the bait. She just sat there at her desk, staring malevolently up at Sheryl. "I do have work to do, Sheryl, so I'd appreciate it if you could tell me whatever it is you're here to tell me, and be on your way."

Sheryl smiled, a completely self-satisfied smile, that she'd thoroughly earned the right to. "It's more show than tell. Like kindergarten. That ought to be about your speed." She put a copy of Vogue down on the desk, opened to the Mirage ad. "I'll just leave it with you. I realize there are a lot of big words, but if you have trouble with them, the pictures should help you out. Have a lovely day, Maribeth."

She turned on her heel and walked out, not waiting for the woman's no doubt angry response.

She desperately wanted to go directly over to the hospital and show the magazine to Jon, but things still weren't right between them. If she were being honest, it probably didn't help that she'd screamed bloody murder at him for offering up her beautiful Hermès scarf as a bribe to that wretched advertising woman.

Granted, it had worked, but, still, Jon was a genius, with a 163 IQ - he'd told her so on one of their early dates - surely he could have come up with some better idea than giving away the best Christmas gift she'd ever received. Doubly so because he'd been the one to give it to her.

He hadn't appreciated the criticism, which had led to another argument, which had led to shouting, and slammed doors and, finally, to her hurling a vase at the wall after he'd stormed out of her apartment. It had shattered into a million pieces, naturally, and nearly a month later, she was still occasionally finding tiny shards in the carper whenever she forgot her slippers in the bedroom and ventured out into the living room in her bare feet.

She couldn't say why she hadn't apologized to him yet. She was still annoyed about the scarf, and she still felt he might have come up with some other option. But she *had* harassed him into coming on the trip in the first place, and he *had* solved her problem.

It would probably take a psychiatrist to delve into her psyche deeply enough to figure it out, which was no help at all since Jon was the only psychiatrist she knew. Anyway, he could apologize too. He'd yelled right back at her, he'd said hurtful things - true things, she had to admit, but hurtful all the same. Even more hurtful because they *were* true, really.

At least it had given her material for her journal. And wasn't the fact that she was still writing in it almost every night proof that she valued his opinions, that she listened to him? Maybe in lieu of the apology she couldn't bring herself to speak, she could simply give him the journal and let him see for himself.

On the other hand, no. She'd written about the scarf incident. At great length. He probably wouldn't take such a gesture in the spirit it was intended.

If she couldn't show off her huge national magazine ad to Jon, she could at least show it off in her own offices. Seeing it in print, maybe in a tasteful framed display in the main lobby, would definitely rally the troops.

When she arrived, she was greeted by Vanessa Jordan, who was - as usual - agitated. "Sheryl, where have you been? You missed the weekly call from Madame Giverny! You know how she gets when she has to wait for anything."

Vanessa was too young to be this excitable, in Sheryl's opinion. As a junior partner, her job was not to worry, or to criticize her senior partner. At least, unlike so many girls just out of college, she did know how to dress appropriately; today she was wearing a very cute skirt and a fantastic blouse that really set off her blue eyes.

"Madame Giverny works until at least six o'clock every night," Sheryl said. It was just ten o'clock here, that made it four in the afternoon in Paris. Plenty of time to call the woman back. "I'll smooth over any ruffled feathers in a few minutes. But before we do that, *voila*!" She held open the magazine, and Vanessa looked it over.

"I have to say, I'm impressed. I didn't think you'd be able to pull it off. I bet Maribeth will blow her top when she sees it."

"I didn't wait around to find out," Sheryl answered. There wouldn't have been any point; Maribeth had many flaws, but she did have enough self-control to avoid embarrassing herself in front of a rival. "Not that she would have let me know how she was feeling anyway. But I'm sure she shut her office door and had a good cry once I was gone."

Vanessa shook her head. "You didn't go over there just to gloat."

"Gloat is such an ugly word. I prefer to think of it as professional courtesy. Sparing her the indignity of finding out her nasty little scheme failed in front of anybody else. Really, it was the kindest thing I could do."

Her junior partner rolled her eyes. "You wouldn't be kind to Maribeth if your life depended on it." She paused a moment, and grinned. "But I would have loved to see her face all the same."

Sheryl was sure they would be seeing her face before too long. No doubt Maribeth was already working on her revenge. But that was a concern for tomorrow; today was a day to enjoy victory. "Let's focus on us right now. See if you can track down Kenny in the maintenance office and have him get this in a frame and hanging on that wall right there." It would look spectacular across from the frosted glass doors. "And order lunch for the staff. The Firehouse Grille, maybe?"

Vanessa ordered beer as well as food. Enough beer that no work got done at Mirage Cosmetics that afternoon, and almost enough beer to make Sheryl temporarily forget that she couldn't share this triumph with the one person she most wanted to.

9.

JON – THEN

It came as no surprise that Bailey's Books and News was sold out of Vogue Magazine. Sheryl had probably camped out there before the doors even opened yesterday.

When he got to his office, he was surprised not to see her there waiting for him, even considering how chilly their relations had been since the train ride back from Manhattan last month. He knew she held grudges; she'd admitted as much on their first official date, and, anyway, the fact that she had three mortal enemies - at least, three that he knew about - testified eloquently to her unwillingness to let bygones be bygones.

Despite that, he'd hoped that they could get past their latest fight. Failing that, he wished that he could get over her, if there was no chance of a healthy relationship. He gave precisely that advice to his patients all the time, and his eight-thirty appointment, Teresa McConnell, was no exception.

Teresa and her husband, Bob, had been having trouble on and off for several months. They both worked here at the hospital - she a nurse, he a doctor - which made things especially awkward. More than once, he'd advised Teresa to take a good hard look at her marriage, to picture what a relationship that made her truly happy might look like, and to be honest about whether or not she and Bob could get there together or not.

It was far easier to dispense such advice than to take it.

Teresa began their session by commenting that, "I haven't seen your girlfriend around lately. Did you finally wise up about her?"

Jon knew that, a couple of years ago, Sheryl had dated Bob McConnell. Bob and Teresa had been separated at the time, but Teresa was still, understandably, none too pleased about it, and made a point of saying so at every convenient opportunity.

"I appreciate your interest in my personal life, but we're here to talk about you, Teresa," he replied. "And in that spirit, how have things been this past week? Have you been keeping up with your journal?" Teresa shook her head. "I know how busy your job keeps you, believe me. And with two kids at home, you don't have much free time there either. I appreciate that. But if you're ever going to come to terms with the issues that are troubling you, you must find the time to reflect on your feelings, outside of the fifty minutes we spend together each week."

She gave him a sad little smile. "I know you're right, Jon. And I know nobody can do it but me."

He smiled back at her. He was certain she heard the advice she gave to her own patients echoed in his words to her. "Exactly right. Speaking of patients, are you off duty today?" He only now thought to wonder about that; she wasn't in her uniform this morning. Instead, she was wearing a green dress that nicely complemented her dark red hair.

"I've got a meeting with Roberta's teacher this morning. I wanted to look more presentable for a change."

The nurses' uniforms at Emerald Falls General were actually reasonably becoming, but he took her point. "Of course. What's the meeting about?"

"Just a regular parent-teacher conference. She's doing fine. Both of the kids are. And Bob, too."

"And you? You never did answer me about how you've been doing this week."

Before she could answer, there was a knock at the door. Teresa's eyes flashed in anger; she knew as well as he did who was most likely knocking.

"Excuse me one moment." Jon got up and locked the door, then he went to his desk, picked up the phone and pushed the button to connect to his secretary. "Monique, unless it's the President of the United States knocking on my door, kindly tell whomever it is to wait and I will see them when my appointment is over."

The walls of his office were relatively, but not completely, soundproof, so while he couldn't hear what Sheryl was saying to Monique on the other side of the door, he could tell for certain that it was her.

Not that he needed to hear her to know that; nobody else would have bolted past Monique to knock when his door was closed during business hours. On the other hand, she *had* knocked rather than just coming straight in, which was her usual practice.

"I'm sorry, Teresa. Let us continue."

They continued for the full fifty minutes and another ten besides. Every so often, through the walls, he could hear Sheryl's theatrical sighs, each one louder than the last. When the clock hit nine-thirty, he finally ended things. "I think we made some real progress today," he said, the same thing he nearly always said whether actual progress had been made or not. Unless the session had been especially upsetting for the patient, Jon considered it better to send them out on a positive note. And today it actually was true.

He considered it a measure of just *how* true it was that, when Teresa saw Sheryl sitting impatiently in the waiting room, she merely shot his possibly-ex girlfriend a thoroughly venomous look on her way out, rather than actively confronting her.

"My next patient appears to be late," Jon told Sheryl, "so come in for a moment."

She did, and closed and locked the door behind her. "What was she so angry about? You're supposed to be making her better, isn't it working?"

Sheryl laid out on the couch. Jon chose not to comment on that, or on the not-at-all-veiled crack about Teresa, or his therapeutic skills, or possibly both. "You realize you're going to have to leave as soon as my nine-thirty shows up. And you also realize, I'm sure, that Teresa blames you for seducing her husband away from her two years ago." It wasn't violating any doctor-patient confidentiality; Sheryl was perfectly well aware of what Teresa thought about her, and why.

"Is it my fault that they separated when their son got sick, and Bob sought comfort in the loving and sympathetic arms of someone else?"

He glared at her.

"Well, yes, obviously I could have said no, but you weren't even in town then, you didn't see how bad things were between them." Something changed in her expression then. Something in her eyes. Almost like a mask dropping. "And it was only a few months after Brad divorced me. I was in a bad place. It wasn't exactly my proudest moment." By her standards, that last sentence was a remarkable confession. "Anyway, it's ancient history now." Clearly it wasn't, either for Teresa or for Sheryl, but there was no point calling her out, especially after admitting something that had to be difficult for her.

"If you're not here for ancient history," he said, already regretting what he was about to ask, "why did you come over?"

She fished into her purse and pulled out a magazine. "I should have come yesterday, the minute I got my copy. Well, copies."

Jon laughed despite himself. "I assumed you bought out every copy at Bailey's."

She stared hard at him now. "You went over to buy it yourself? Really?"

This, right here, the look in her eyes right now - that was why he couldn't get over her, why it was worth fighting with her, and about her, and sometimes even at her side. Nobody - not his parents, not his brother, not any of his exes, had ever looked at him the way that Sheryl was now. And he doubted there was another person on Earth who ever could.

"How could I not?"

"Especially since you had a small part in making sure my ads actually ran." She said it with a perfectly straight face, but he saw the twinkle in her eyes. This was the Sheryl he'd fallen in love with, even if he'd never properly said those three little words, in the right order.

He could say them now. Nothing would be easier. Three simple words, and the first of them was on the tip of his tongue when the door opened and his nine-thirty walked in.

10.

ARIEL - NOW

"So, whatever happened to that Maribeth woman?" Ariel had heard her name mentioned every once in a while, in passing, in the same way that her parents talked about people they'd known in college or second cousins who'd send a Christmas card once every five years or so. But she was a major character in the diary; Maribeth Peale and her many sins showed up on almost every page.

Her mother made a face; the same face she used to make when Sigmund was a puppy and had an accident on the living room rug. "She moved away, what, fifteen years ago? And good riddance to bad rubbish when she did, too."

Her father refilled her mother's glass and put an arm around her. "As you've read, your mother and Ms. Peale were not exactly the best of friends. There were some rather ugly moments, and their feud went on until just before you were born, in fact."

The math didn't add up. If Maribeth had moved away in 2003 or so, that meant she'd been in Emerald Falls for six years after Ariel herself had been born. "So, after you had me, you just decided to bury the hatchet, Mom? No offense, but that doesn't really sound like you."

Her mother wasn't offended. "It's not." That was one of the things Ariel admired most about her. She might say or do just about anything, but she'd usually own up to it. "But when I had you - really, the moment I went into labor - I realized there was something more important than me and my feelings."

Her father wagged a finger. "We said the *whole* truth, Sheryl."

She downed her wine before responding to that, then took a deep breath. "Do you really want to tell her that story, too?"

"What story?" She'd read the whole diary, but it only went up to April 1, 1997 - the day her mother had told her father she was pregnant. Of course Mom would have done that on April fool's day. And there was no story anywhere in there that seemed like it could have led to a lasting truce between her and Maribeth.

For his part, her father seemed to be rethinking things. "Maybe we're getting ahead of ourselves here. Let's get her born before we tell her what happened on her second birthday and why Maribeth still sends her a card every year."

"What?" Ariel and her mother said it in unison. Her mother looked – this was the first time in Ariel's life the word actually fit the circumstances – gobsmacked.

"She's never - I never - we never got any cards from that woman!"

Her father smiled, a little sadly. "Even after what happened, I didn't think you'd appreciate the gesture from her. Anyway, she didn't sign her name, she just signed the cards 'Auntie Em' and used a post office box for the return address. She did sign the checks, though."

"What?" Again, mother and daughter spoke together.

"She's been sending you five hundred dollars every birthday, and a thousand on your sixteenth. I deposited it all straight into your college fund."

It made no sense. "Why would she do that if she hated Mom so much?"

Her mother finally had an answer, and an expression that Ariel rarely saw on her face – genuine regret. "She didn't hate you, honey." She said it grudgingly, looking like she couldn't quite believe the words coming out of her mouth. "Nobody did. Nobody could ever hate you." That wasn't true, but then again, good luck getting through high school without *somebody* hating you. "And after what happened when you were two, well, I guess maybe she really was sort of human underneath it all, and, I don't know, I suppose she felt a special connection with you."

"But why?"

"All in good time," her father said. "I apologize for the spoilers, but we should tell everything in order. I know you like to skip ahead to the end of the book, just like your mother, but not this time. So," he grinned, "where were we?"

Her mother seemed to be recovering from the shock of discovering that one of her nemeses had actually done something kind. "You were about to tell me you loved me, when we were rudely interrupted by one of your patients, if I recall correctly..."

11.

SHERYL - THEN

They'd had a moment. Well, they'd almost had one, anyway. There they were, everything was back to normal, all was seemingly forgiven, and Jon was about to - well, she hoped he was about to say something that she needed desperately to hear, and then Bella Travers had to come in for her appointment.

Why did Bella even need to see a psychiatrist anyway? She had a perfect life. She had money, and a great wardrobe, and two healthy, reasonably well-behaved kids, and an attentive husband who was really quite attractive.

Oh, well. There'd be another time, another moment. Maybe even tonight. In the meantime, though, she did have work to do back at the office.

Unfortunately, there was something else waiting for her when she got back to Mirage. Someone else. A tall woman with severely short blonde hair, a perpetual sneer on her face, and more money than God.

"Annalise, what a pleasant surprise to see you here!"

Annalise was the eldest of Noah Starwood's three children, and his equal – if not his superior – in ruthlessness. She was sitting in Sheryl's custom-ordered ergonomic office chair, her feet up on Sheryl's imported, hand-finished oak desk, those feet clad in a pair of red Manolo Blahniks that cost more than Sheryl's monthly mortgage payment.

Maybe two payments.

"Well. It *is* a pleasure that you showed up, rather than slinking away from me like a whipped dog." Had she known Annalise would be waiting for her, she *would* have slunk away. Possibly while whimpering in a high-pitched sort of way that might be mistaken for a distressed poodle.

Someone really should have warned her. She'd have to have words with Alexis. Or was it Alexa? Maybe Allison? Something starting with an A, anyway. Whatever her name was, the new girl the temp agency sent over was falling down on the job. She couldn't hold a candle to Lucinda, who was a top-notch receptionist, except she had to go and get herself married and pregnant and leave Sheryl in the lurch. She supposed she shouldn't blame the woman too much, though. The heart wanted what the heart wanted, didn't it?

"I do not slink," Sheryl answered, trying to match Annalise's tone. She was proud of herself for even getting close. "But that's neither here nor there. What brings you to my office this morning?"

As if it was a question. This month's Vogue was on the desk, open to the big two-page Mirage ad.

"I'll be honest," Annalise said. Sheryl desperately wanted to point out that it was easy to be honest when, first of all, you didn't care what anyone else thought, and, second, you had the full power and resources of Starwood Industries behind you, so you didn't have to care anyway. But she thought better of it and let Annalise go on. "I could care less about your advertising, your company, or you personally. Mirage Cosmetics isn't even a speck on the radar for my family's company, and on a personal level, despite your many flaws, you were far from the worst sister-in-law my idiot brothers have saddled the family with over the years."

From anyone else, that would have been insulting, but for Annalise, it was as close as she'd probably ever come to saying something nice about her. "So why are you here?"

"As I said, I don't care about the advertising. My younger brother, however, for reasons best known to himself, cares a great deal about Maribeth Peale. So much so that he gave her half of his shares in Starwood Industries as an engagement gift. And Ms. Peale, for reasons that I'm sure you are quite familiar with, despises you and wants your company destroyed."

It all made sense now. She'd assumed that Maribeth had instigated the effort to get her ads pulled, and had somehow convinced Noah Starwood to do her dirty work, and she couldn't come up with any good reason why Noah would have gone along with it.

But it hadn't been Noah, it had been Annalise. And the shares that had been gifted to Maribeth explained it all. In her brief time as a member of both the Starwood family, and the board of Starwood Industries, she'd seen up close how their family business was run. The company was entirely family-owned, but the shares were divided between Noah, his wife, his children and the one daughter-in-law he'd ever approved of. And although the family put on a united front against the rest of the world, they were far from united behind the scenes. Every board vote was an extended and often ugly negotiation, mostly among Noah's children, who for the most part had never really gotten along.

Putting even a small amount of company stock in Maribeth's hands could have made her the deciding vote. And if Annalise wanted something, and needed that deciding vote, she wouldn't hesitate to use her power to crush a company that wasn't even a speck on her radar to get it.

"I can see how that would make things difficult for you."

Annalise smiled; it was the sort of smile that Jaws probably displayed right before he chowed down on some poor oblivious swimmer. "It's not difficult for me at all. I made a couple of phone calls to stop your ads being run, because I assumed, mistakenly as it turned out, that you would be easily dealt with." The smile was still there, still the most predatory thing Sheryl had ever seen. "My mistake. I won't make it again. But because I am a reasonable person, and because I believe in expending my time and energy on important matters rather than trivial details, I'm going to give you an opportunity to resolve the situation for me."

That sounded ominous, but Sheryl had just enough of a survival instinct not to say so. "Obviously I'd like to help you however I can."

"Good." Annalise still wore the Jaws smile. This felt like the moment where Roy Scheider - or was it Richard Dreyfuss? she couldn't remember - remarked that they would need a bigger boat. "I expected you would. There is a Starwood board meeting next Monday, at nine AM sharp. Exactly one week from now. At that meeting there will be a vote which is vital to my interests, and those of the family generally. You have until that meeting convenes to make sure Maribeth's shares vote the way I wish them to."

How on Earth was she supposed to accomplish that? "Of course, Annalise. I'll do it. Just put it right out of your mind."

"I will." The shark had eaten its fill, and was satisfied. For now. "I will assume that the vote will go my way with no unexpected difficulties next Monday morning. If it does not...well, there's no need for ugly threats, is there? We're both mature adults, and we both understand precisely what will happen if things do not go as they should." Annalise removed her legs from the desk, and made a show of brushing herself off as she stood up. Sheryl stepped aside and let her walk past and out of the office.

"By the way, Sheryl, there's an appallingly large dust bunny under your desk. I'd be happy to recommend a new cleaning service for you, assuming you're still in business next week. Good day."

Sheryl watched her go, and waited until she'd disappeared into the elevator before closing and locking her office door. When she sat down in her chair, she noticed that her hands were shaking. This was not a good way to start the workday. Not at all.

Worst of all, Annalise was right. There *was* a huge dust bunny under her desk. As if she didn't have enough problems already.

12.

JON - THEN

The last patient of the day was gone. He'd had several good sessions today, a couple of them quite intense, and he was grateful that they'd been so intense because they'd taken his mind off of what he'd almost said to Sheryl this morning.

As he tidied up and handled some paperwork, he went over that conversation, and his feelings, again. He'd been so overcome with what he'd seen in her eyes that he'd allowed himself to completely forget about all the maddening things Sheryl had said, and done, over the past almost eight months.

Maybe it was time to do what he'd told Teresa McConnell to do. Try to picture what a healthy relationship with Sheryl would look like, and figure out if there was any way to get there.

He could picture her in the Chalet. She'd helped decorate it, so it already had her feel in almost every room. There was more than enough closet space for the both of them, even considering her voluminous wardrobe. The idea of her doing unnatural things to his precious kitchen appliances was troubling, but at the end of the day, they were only machines, and if need be, he could buy the extended warranty plan for all of them.

Those were all surface things, though. What would it look like to have a relationship with Sheryl that had healthy boundaries, with real give and take, with true respect for the other, with honest-to-goodness selflessness on both sides?

If he was being truly honest with himself - and what was the point of the exercise if he wasn't? - he had never experienced that in any of his own prior relationships. And he knew for a fact that Sheryl hadn't, either.

But did that mean they couldn't learn?

He hoped they could. And maybe hope was, if not enough, at least a good place to start from.

They could begin over dinner, except he couldn't reach her.

She wasn't answering her direct line at the office. Angela, the new receptionist, wasn't picking up at the switchboard. Sheryl's home phone rang five times before the answering machine clicked on, and her cell phone went straight to voicemail. That, at least, was neither a surprise nor cause for concern; the woman habitually forgot to recharge the thing. But the fact that she wasn't reachable anywhere was a little worrying.

Obviously, she could be in her car, or in the shower after a taxing day of work. On the other hand, it was probably best not to dwell on the image of her in the shower just at the moment.

Anyway, there were a dozen completely reasonable and innocuous explanations for her inability to be reached. But in his experience, when Sheryl went radio silent, it was rarely reasonable or innocuous.

———

As it turned out, she found him. Since his espresso machine was still awaiting repair, he'd walked over to Krista's Koffee Hut on Third St for a proper cup of coffee to reward himself for a good day's therapy.

He was chatting with Krista over a cup of her special Aztec Blend when Sheryl walked in. Or, more accurately, stormed in.

"Jon! I've been looking all over town for you! What are you doing *here*?" There was a thoroughly ominous emphasis on "here." Then she took note of Krista. "And what are you doing talking to *her*?"

He'd told Sheryl, more than once, that jealousy was an unattractive emotion. And unfounded jealousy, as Sheryl's attitude towards Krista was, was poisonous, and in the end it only harmed the individual who was jealous. Clearly his words had not stuck with her.

"I'm enjoying a well-deserved cup of coffee. I had a very successful day, and I helped several patients, thank you for asking." For her part, Krista was holding back laughter, which he appreciated. He doubted that Sheryl would take being laughed at very well just now.

"Do you want to know how my day went?" It wasn't really a question, and he didn't bother to answer it. "I had Annalise Starwood waiting for me. In my office. In my *chair*. Making death threats."

Now Krista did laugh. "Death threats?"

"You can laugh!" Sheryl turned on the owner of the coffee shop. "Nobody is marching into this little shack and telling you they're going to murder your insignificant hobby of a business if you don't do what they tell you, are they? No, they're not! If you had a mortal threat to your livelihood, to everything you've spent years building up, nurturing like it was your own child, maybe you'd understand."

Prone though Sheryl was to exaggeration, Jon was sure she had been visited by Annalise Starwood. And there was no getting around it: the only Starwood daughter was terrifying when she wanted to be. Which was most of the time. Still, there was no call to lash out at poor Krista like that.

He beckoned for Sheryl to sit down; in his experience, it was harder to be outraged when you were sitting, preferably with a nice, calming cup of tea. "Krista, could you make Sheryl a large lavender tea, and put it on my bill?"

Krista left without a further word. "You shouldn't have yelled at her, Sheryl. It's not her fault that Annalise visited you."

"Visited? She was there waiting like a spider in the web. And it was my web she was waiting in! Do you have any idea what it's like to walk into your office and have someone who shouldn't be there looking up at you from your own desk?" Jon didn't respond to that; he was proud that he didn't even roll his eyes, but only gave her the tiniest of sighs. Agitated as she was, she got the hint. "Yes, well, that's not the same thing at all. I'm someone you want to see. It's a pleasant surprise when I'm waiting in your office. Seeing her there was like coming home and there's Hannibal Lecter sitting on your couch and reading your newspaper and wearing your slippers. How would you feel about that?"

Both a spider and Hannibal Lecter were reasonable comparisons for Annalise Starwood. He couldn't really argue that. "It would be disconcerting, I agree. So what did she want with you? What threats did she make?"

Sheryl proceeded to recap the entire saga of the Vogue Magazine ads, either forgetting or not caring that he'd had a front row seat to most of it. By the time she got to what Annalise said, Krista had returned with the tea. Sheryl stopped talking long enough to take a sip and comment that, "Your coffee tastes different today, maybe you should check the machine." Jon shot a momentary glance at Krista, who was, again, struggling to hold back laughter. Sheryl didn't even notice; she just downed most of the rest of her drink in one long swallow. Then she returned to her tale.

"So Annalise said that Maribeth tricked Will Starwood into giving her control of his shares of the family stock, and she needed those votes at the next board meeting, and she gave me a week to make sure the vote goes her way, or else she'll destroy Mirage. And me. And probably you, Doc, just because we're - well, whatever it is that we are now."

Krista appeared interested despite herself. "How are you going to get Maribeth to vote the way Annalise wants?"

Sheryl shook her head. "How should I know? If I had the answer, do you think I'd be drowning my sorrows with this terrible coffee? And the least you could have done was put some rum or Baileys or something in it. I'm in the middle of a life-and-death crisis here!"

It might not be life-or-death, but Jon couldn't deny that it was definitely a crisis for Mirage Cosmetics. The Starwoods were not known for making idle threats. On the other hand, though, it didn't add up. "Why did Annalise even come to you in the first place?" Sheryl looked at him with disbelief. "What I mean is, while I've never personally been in her crosshairs, her reputation definitely precedes her, and from everything I've heard, she's not one to let anybody else do her dirty work."

Krista agreed. "When she wants you stabbed in the back, she likes to stick the knife in herself."

A thought occurred to Jon then, and he spoke it more to himself than to his companions. "Will no one rid me of this turbulent priest?"

Both women stared at him. Krista was completely at a loss, and Sheryl was annoyed. "What does Henry the Eighth have to do with anything?"

He had to give her credit for being close. It was the wrong king, but she had the right monarchy, at least. "Henry the Second, actually." To Krista, he added, "according to legend, or at least Shakespeare, Henry said it, and some of his knights overheard him and took it as an order to kill Thomas Becket."

Comprehension dawned on Sheryl's face. "You think Annalise was ordering me to kill Maribeth?" She looked almost hopeful at the thought.

"I'm sure she didn't mean that," Krista said, although she didn't sound terribly sure.

"I doubt she was ordering a murder, no," Jon said. "But clearly she has issues with Maribeth, and for whatever reason she can't resolve them herself, so she's pushing it off on you, Sheryl."

Perhaps it was that she simply couldn't be seen to move openly against her brother's fiancée. Sibling relations were complicated enough on their own, and no doubt more so when there were millions of dollars involved.

"Well, if I can't kill her, what am I supposed to do to get Maribeth to do what Annalise wants her to?"

Krista shook her head in mock sadness, her blonde curls bouncing all around. "I don't know, but you'd better figure it out before Annalise squashes you like a bug. Which would be a shame. I really like that new mascara you came out with last Christmas."

Sheryl had been rude to Krista first; Jon couldn't really begrudge her a little jab in response. But he had no wish to play referee between two women who honestly had no reason to be fighting.

"Ladies, if we could keep things civil. And that means you, too, Sheryl. We're all adults here. And anyway, we've hogged this table long enough." He stood up to leave, and Sheryl hopped up an instant later.

"I would say it's been fun, but the Doc here keeps telling me how important honesty is. Bye, Krista."

To her credit, though, when they were about half a block down the street, she admitted, "Maybe that was a little bit unfair. Other than the horrible coffee, I guess she didn't really do anything wrong."

<hr />

Sheryl's behavior at the Koffee Hut cast doubt on his feelings about the healthy relationship he hoped they could build. But he followed her up to her apartment anyway; she was obviously very rattled over the meeting with Annalise Starwood. He didn't have the heart to leave her alone, but it was also a matter of public safety. In her agitated state, Heaven only knew what Sheryl might decide to do, or whom to do it to.

"I like the new vase," he commented when he stepped into the apartment.

"I thought it was time for a change, you know?" He'd heard the old vase smash against the wall immediately after he'd slammed the door behind him the last time he'd been here. But there was no point bringing up such a sordid detail.

"There were some lovely orchids at that nursery on Highway 9, you know the one I mean. I think they'd look spectacular in that vase, especially if you moved it so it catches the afternoon sun." His mother had been a decorator, and though he'd never been particularly interested in the field, he'd inherited a bit of her eye for design.

"You could have bought me one."

"I didn't know you had a new vase to put one in. And we haven't exactly been on the best of terms lately." Anger flashed in her eyes, but she didn't immediately respond; instead she took a deep breath. That was certainly progress on her part. "Forgive me, that was uncalled for. Regardless of what happened the last time we were together in your apartment, we are here now, and if I can, I would like to try and help you with your Annalise problem."

"Believe it or not, I appreciate it." She scoffed. "But unless you've got a magic wand or a Delorean you never told me about, I'm not sure how you can help me."

"I've got neither, I'm afraid." He wasn't sure what an old car from a bankrupt company had to do with anything; no doubt it was a reference to some movie or TV show he'd missed during the five years he'd spent in Vienna working on his doctorate. It didn't really matter anyway. "But I do have years of psychiatric training, and a willing spirit. That ought to be good for something, don't you think?"

13.

ARIEL - NOW

"Dad, do you seriously not know about *Back to the Future*?" Her father had always a little bit stuffy and oblivious to popular culture, but that was ridiculous.

"Of course I do, Ariel. Although I did miss it when it first came out. Your mother rented it around Christmastime that year and made me watch it."

"Rented it? You mean, like, you went someplace and got a DVD?"

Her mother laughed. "I mean, like, a VHS tape. I went to Blockbuster, they were really big back then, and I got the tape and stuck it in, like, an actual VCR, and we watched it over several glasses of eggnog."

It was probably the same VCR that was hidden away in the attic, brought down and plugged in once a year or so -

usually around her birthday, come to think of it - to watch home videos of her as a toddler.

Her mother's old cell phone was up there, too. The thing was huge; it weighed at least two pounds, if not more. But that was her mother, never throwing anything away if she could possibly avoid it.

As interesting as old movies were, *Back to the Future* was a distraction from the real story. "So, what did you end up doing to help Annalise?" She gestured to the diary. "You were kind of vague about exactly how that all went down, Mom."

"Yes," her father agreed. "You were rather vague. And we did promise our daughter the whole truth, did we not?"

"Are you really going to make me tell it?"

Ariel and her father answered together: "Yes!"

14.

SHERYL - THEN

What a complete waste of time last night had been. Jon had spent nearly three hours in her apartment, on her imported sofa, not more than a foot away from her, and not only hadn't he touched her, he'd also contributed exactly nothing in the way of helpful ideas about dealing with the Annalise situation.

Maybe he'd been right back at the Koffee Hut after all. Maybe Annalise really had been asking her to murder Maribeth.

Not that she honestly wanted to do that. She despised the woman, true. She wanted to punch the woman's lights out pretty much every time they crossed paths, true. But real, permanent physical harm? That was a whole other thing. Sheryl was fairly certain she wasn't capable of that. Not in cold blood, not merely to deal with a business dispute.

Annalise Starwood, on the other hand, probably was capable of it. Just in the few years since she'd come to Emerald Falls, Sheryl knew of at least three suspicious deaths that were connected to the Starwood family. And Annalise's eyes were cold and dead, exactly like the Komodo Dragons in that nature show she'd watched a few months back. It had been both fascinating and horrifying: the giant lizards bit their prey, passed along dozens of toxic bacteria, and then sat back and waited for their victim to die so they could feast.

Actually, the lizards' eyes had more life in them than Annalise's did. And yet she was asking Sheryl to deal with Maribeth rather than taking out her own trash.

Why?

The answer came to her suddenly, and it was so obvious that she cursed herself for wasting the whole day trying to come up with it. If Maribeth was threatened, or harmed, or blackmailed or anything else untoward, she would run immediately to her fiancé. And Will would assume - correctly - that it was Annalise's doing. That would harden both his and Maribeth's attitude, and it might even push Annalise's other brother - Sheryl's own ex-husband Brad - to join with them against Annalise.

But if she, Sheryl, went directly after Will Starwood, well, that would just be viewed as within her normal range of behavior, wouldn't it? She had briefly dated Will a while back, hadn't she? Would it really surprise anybody if she made another play for him?

If she could cause a rift between Will and Maribeth, that would cancel out the woman's votes next week, wouldn't it? Or, maybe, if the rift was bad enough, the engagement might be called off entirely and the shares might revert back to Will, who could then be counted on to do what his sister wanted. Even if he didn't, Annalise couldn't reasonably expect her to do anything further once Maribeth was out of the picture.

With that moment of revelation came another. Sheryl understood why that course of action hadn't occurred to her while Jon was here. Because he would hate it.

No, hate wasn't nearly a strong enough word. Loathe didn't even really properly describe how he would feel about the idea of her flirting with Will Starwood in order to get Annalise off her back. Especially when mere flirting might not be enough to do the trick. Even if they weren't officially dating right now, they both knew – or at least hoped, or at least she hoped he hoped - it was inevitable, and it wasn't unreasonable for him to be unhappy at the prospect of her potentially kissing another man. It wouldn't matter to him that it would only be for professional purposes.

"Wow, even in my head, that sounded awful," she said. She was in her bedroom, and now she was talking to herself, which wasn't a good sign. The woman looking back at her in the full-length mirror didn't say anything in response, but Sheryl could see that she, too, disapproved of the idea, and that was a worse sign.

"What are you looking at? If you've got something to say, say it!" Her reflection still didn't answer. If Sheryl couldn't even get *herself* to go along with this, then it truly was a terrible, horrible, no good, very bad plan, even by her standards. But what other choice did she have?

She put the plan in motion the next day.

On Wednesday nights, the Firehouse Grille had live music, and to the disgust of his father, siblings and, Sheryl presumed, fiancée, Will Starwood played in a band.

More than played; he was the lead singer of Pay the Bill, which she had to admit was a clever name. She wasn't particularly fond of their music; they mostly did covers of stuff like Eddie Money, and the occasional Bon Jovi song. Their rendition of *Living on a Prayer* was almost tolerable, but that was as far as Sheryl was willing to go.

Personally, she was more of a disco girl herself. Her fondest musical memory was the ABBA concert she'd gone to back in 1979, during the semester she'd spent studying abroad in Europe. But for the purpose of saving her business, she could pretend to enjoy Will's singing.

At three o'clock, Will was there, working on the setup for tonight's show. He wore a ratty t-shirt and ripped jeans; it probably took a week off of Noah Starwood's life every time he saw his son and potential heir dressed like that. For her part, Sheryl was impressed that he was doing the grunt work himself rather than leaving it to his bandmates.

"Will!" She called out to him from across the restaurant. "You know, in the right light, you sort of look like Jon Bon Jovi."

That was a ridiculous lie; Will was handsome enough, but he looked absolutely nothing like the rock star in question. Still, it got his attention and earned her a devilish grin.

"I don't know about that, but let me tell you, I'd give anything to play one show in front of a crowd like he gets. Can you imagine, fifty thousand people, all there for you?"

She could imagine it. She *had* imagined it, many times. In her dream, though, it wasn't a concert. It was a convention. Maybe a huge Tony Robbins style event, and she'd been invited to speak to talk about how she'd turned Mirage Cosmetics into a worldwide success and what all those thousands of hopeful people in the crowd could learn from her example.

"You never know, Will. Maybe you'll hit it big like that. Anything can happen." He probably did know, though. If he really had the talent to be a huge star, the Starwoods would have put their money and power behind him. As much as they disapproved of his music, if it could have increased the family fortune, they'd all have held their noses and cashed the checks.

Except Maribeth, probably. She wouldn't want to share Will with anyone, certainly not legions of adoring fans, or bandmates who might tempt her fiancé astray while on tour. Had Maribeth ever seen him perform? If she hadn't, tonight's show might be a good way to start undermining their relationship.

"You going to come tonight? It's going to be a good show."

Yes. Yes, she was. "I might even bring a friend or two."

"Vanessa, do you have any friends?"

Her junior partner glared at her. "First of all, yes, obviously. Second of all, whatever it is you want, the answer is no. I haven't forgotten the 'free samples' you asked me to give out for the Illusions of Beauty campaign last fall."

"It's nothing like that." Anyway, the rashes had gone away after a couple of weeks, what was the big deal?

Vanessa was still glaring. Sheryl gave the girl her brightest, most earnest smile and pressed on. "Seriously. It's completely harmless. And it'll even be fun. Just round up as many of your friends as you can get on short notice, and bring them over to the Firehouse Grille tonight. You can pay the cover charge for all of them out of petty cash." A whole gaggle of young women ooh-ing and aah-ing at Will was sure to raise Maribeth's blood pressure. "And tell them to wear the tightest, most revealing things they've got in their closets. The things their mothers would never let them wear out in public. You too. That leather miniskirt you've got would be perfect tonight."

Vanessa looked as though she wasn't sure whether to be amused or appalled. "What's this about, Sheryl?"

"It's about you and your friends having a good time. You're so serious, you work much too hard."

Vanessa's eyes narrowed. "Someone has to around here. And I know you're cooking something up, I just can't begin to guess what it is."

"It's all in a good cause. Just get as many girls as you can, as sexy as they can make themselves, and, what the heck, I'll even buy the first round of drinks."

15.

JON - THEN

Jon wasn't sure what possessed him to come to the Firehouse Grille on a Wednesday night. Sheryl commented often enough about him needing to get out more, meet his fellow citizens and "become a part of the community." Maybe her words had been working away in his subconscious and they finally bore fruit tonight. Or maybe he just wanted a good, old-fashioned greasy burger and fries.

The problem was that the Grille had a band on Wednesday nights. He didn't have any particular objection to live music, but he generally preferred a string quartet, or, if he was in the mood for big and loud, a trip to Manhattan and a concert from the New York Philharmonic. Maybe even, on very special occasions, if he really wanted to treat himself, the Metropolitan Opera.

He had very little use for rock music, or pop, or whatever you could call it that Will Starwood and his band were playing tonight. Jon came in just as they were finishing a song he didn't recognize, which was hardly surprising.

Jon found a table in the back corner, as far away from the band as it was possible to get, and with great difficulty managed to get the attention of a waitress. She arrived just as the next song began, and even with him shouting, she was unable to understand what he was saying. He finally resorted to pantomiming drinking from a wineglass. Since he'd never been good at charades, though, God only knew what she would actually bring him to drink.

He hadn't been here for many live music nights, but in his limited experience this crowd was the biggest and liveliest one he'd seen. Right up front, only a few feet from the band, there was a whole group of young women, all of whom were scantily dressed, most of whom appeared to be thoroughly drunk. He thought he recognized a couple of them from Sheryl's office, and, right there, at the table nearest the kitchen door, in the leather miniskirt, wasn't that her partner Vanessa?

Yes, it was. And right next to her, in a much-too-short red dress that made his heart skip a beat, was Sheryl herself.

She hadn't seen him; she seemed to be focused entirely on the stage, entirely on Will Starwood and his ridiculous "artistically" torn jeans and t-shirt that probably hadn't been washed in weeks. Or possibly months.

All the women in that gaggle - there was no more suitable word for them - were focused on Will, and shouting along with the chorus of the song. He did know this one; it was a cover of a song he'd never liked very much. Jon could understand why Will had it in his act, though. It had to be a nice boost to the ego to have dozens of attractive women calling for him to "take me home tonight."

It called to mind a patient he'd had back when he'd been doing his training, in Vienna. One of the first patients he'd seen on his own, in fact. He was a touring American rock star, and Jon had done several sessions with him. Near the end of the last one, the man had talked about the women who threw themselves at musicians.

"The groupies," he'd said, "I know, they hate when you call 'em that, but I gotta call a spade a spade, right, man? The groupies, there ain't nothing like them." Then he'd looked Jon up and down critically, which had been disconcerting, and said, "you'd do pretty good with them. They dig the hair, man, and you got that down. One word of advice, if you go for it, make sure you got a good doctor on speed dial. You never know when you'll need penicillin at two o'clock in the morning." Jon had not, of course, "gone for it," but, to his everlasting shame, he had bought a couple of hundred dollars worth of hair care products shortly after that last session.

Will presumably wasn't going to "go for it" either, not with a fiancée - an extremely wealthy fiancée at that - waiting for him at home.

Except Maribeth Peale wasn't waiting for him at home. She was here, standing just inside the front door of the restaurant, staring at the stage in either disbelief or horror; Jon couldn't quite tell from thirty or so feet away.

She stood there, rooted to the spot, and despite the distance, Jon could see very clearly the way her expression was changing to one he could definitely recognize: barely controlled rage.

And then the song ended, and one of the girls up front - thankfully not Sheryl - ran up to Will, threw her arms around his neck and kissed him, hard. And Maribeth's barely controlled rage became thoroughly uncontrolled.

"Maribeth, please calm down." Luckily for her, Will Starwood didn't seem to have seen her punch out the waiter who'd been unlucky enough to try and take her drink order at the exact moment her fiancé was kissing someone else in front of the whole crowd.

"I am calm!"

"Your face would not be purple if you were calm. Now let's just take a walk and try to take a few deep breaths and we can talk about this rationally." He had a firm grip on her arm, and he was trying his best to steer her away from the restaurant.

"There's nothing rational about what I just saw!"

No, there really wasn't. "Be that as it may, a little walk will do you good. Besides, the manager said that as long as you don't try to come back in tonight, the waiter won't press charges, and they won't permanently ban you from the place. I think that's quite fair, all things considered."

Maribeth turned on him, eyes blazing. "What do you know about fair? Your girlfriend set that whole scene up!"

He began to say that, no, of course Sheryl hadn't done that. But the truth was, it was *exactly* the sort of thing she would do. Especially now, under orders from Annalise Starwood to do something about Maribeth's possession of Starwood family stock. And whether she had planned it or not it had worked like a charm.

"I don't know anything about what Sheryl did or didn't do." Had a patient given him that answer in a session, he'd have called them out for being evasive. He owed her something a little better. "But I would have done everything in my power to put a stop to it if I knew she was planning anything." That was absolutely true, but still of only limited value; there wasn't much he - or anyone - could do to stop Sheryl Jones when she made her mind up to do something. No matter how reckless or ill-advised it was.

Actually, the more reckless and ill-advised it was, the more committed she was to it. Which was unhealthy and self-sabotaging, and yet, somehow, a part of her charm. Jon couldn't say why he felt that way, and he had no wish to interrogate his own unconscious desires and feelings to find out, however unhealthy and self-sabotaging it was to be attracted to exactly those characteristics in someone else. At any rate, that didn't matter now. Maribeth was the one who was having a crisis, and as a doctor, he had a responsibility to help.

He walked her past the fire station, then up Fourth St. He had no destination in mind, other than getting her away from the scene of the crime. As they went, she asked him, "Why are you even bothering? Your girlfriend hates me. She won't thank you for spending time with me." Her tone implied that she wouldn't be thanking him either.

"First of all," he answered, "I don't allow Sheryl, or anyone else for that matter, to choose my friends for me."

She didn't quite smile. "So, we're friends?"

Jon wasn't prepared to go quite that far; Sheryl aside, he didn't really know Maribeth very well. "Well, we're not enemies."

"What are we, exactly?"

He gave her a rueful smile. "How about two civilized adults who travel in similar circles having a calm, rational conversation. As civilized adults are sometimes known to do."

She laughed, finally. "I've got to give you points for tact, if nothing else. I suppose they taught you that in Vienna." For an instant he wondered how she knew he'd studied there, but she of course she'd seen his resume when she interviewed him along with the rest of the hospital board. "Actually, a calm, rational conversation would be nice. I don't get to have that many of them, to be honest."

Between her rivalry with Sheryl, her involvement with the Starwood family, and the simultaneously petty and cutthroat politics of the hospital board, he could believe that. "I'm glad to be of service, then." They crossed Hull St., and Jon gazed upwards at the Parkview Towers building looming above him. "This is your building, right?"

"Sixteenth floor." She pointed up. "Right there, that's me." Jon would have to take her word for it; it was too dark, and the window she pointed at too high up, for him to be able to see anything. "You know, I can see the Chalet from my bedroom window." Just like Sheryl could. "I was surprised when you rented it. Nobody lived there for a couple of years before you. The story is, it's haunted."

He had heard that, but he'd never heard - or bothered to look into - the story. Every town had a legend about a house or building that was haunted, after all. Maribeth didn't seem the type to put much stock in urban legends.

"Really."

"I don't know the whole history," she said as they walked along Hull St. "But the last family that lived there, the Kellys, the daughter got sick, and nobody could diagnose what it was, and after she died, the wife just disappeared one night, and a couple of days later, the husband went over the cliff." The Chalet was only a mile or so east of the falls that gave the town its name, and it was right on the edge of a cliff overlooking the land between the twin lakes - Tristan and Isolde. Whoever named them had clearly had a strange sense of humor.

"Is that true?"

"Cross my heart," Maribeth said. "You can ask anybody. The only thing people disagree on is whether the husband jumped off the cliff, or if he just fell."

There was another possibility, of course. "Or maybe he was pushed."

Maribeth nodded. "Could be. Like I said, I had only just come to town, so I didn't know the Kellys." They were just now passing the business that had, presumably, once belonged to that unfortunate family, Kelly's Gas and Go. "But speaking of throwing people off a cliff, I have to ask you, how do you stand being around that woman? I'll admit that she's not unattractive when she makes an effort, but how can someone as intelligent and civilized as you tolerate her?"

He'd known the conversation would come back around to Sheryl. And, honestly, he had been asking himself a similar question over the past few weeks. But he wasn't going to get into it with Sheryl's archenemy. "That's a matter for her and me. All I will say is that you don't know everything about her, any more than she does about you. Actually, I will say one more thing. I think you two may have more in common than either of you realizes."

As he said it, he realized it was probably even more true than he'd initially thought. The differences between the two women were mainly stylistic. They were both fearless, both very ambitious, both unwilling to let any obstacle stand in the way of what they wanted. The main thing that Sheryl had and Maribeth didn't was a willingness to be vulnerable, and to wear her heart on her sleeve - except that phrase didn't really begin to do her justice.

They were walking down Third St. now, and just a few paces ahead, there was the Firehouse Grille again. "I'll give you one thing we have in common," Maribeth said. "Sheryl and I both know how to recognize a good man when we see one."

They turned the corner onto Galley St., now only ten feet or so from the front entrance of the Grille. People were coming out; they must have been walking for longer than Jon had realized, if the concert was over already.

He was about to suggest to Maribeth that, since the place had quieted down, they might have a quick meal before heading their separate ways for the evening. Before he could, though, she stopped in her tracks, turned to him, threw her arms around his neck, and kissed him like there was no tomorrow.

16.

ARIEL - NOW

Ariel was stunned at the thought that her mother's mortal enemy had kissed her father, and her mother hadn't even written about it in her diary. But there was something else that she needed an answer about first.

"You guys never told me the house was haunted! Somebody went over the cliff right outside? That's, like, the creepiest thing ever!"

Her father held up a hand. "What Maribeth said wasn't exactly true."

Her mother snorted. "Yeah, there's a shock."

"Mom, be nice! She's been sending me five hundred bucks a year." Besides, even her mother ought to be able to let a grudge go when the target hadn't been in her life for fifteen years.

Her mother didn't quite laugh, but she did have the good grace to look embarrassed. "You're right, Ariel. And I guess I can try to be fair. She wasn't lying, not about that story, anyway. She really believed it. I did, too, to be honest. Just about everyone did."

That made no sense. She knew her father was not superstitious, but she still had trouble imagining that he would have moved into a house where the previous family had suffered such an awful fate.

Unless he hadn't known. "Except Dad, because you didn't tell him when you suggested the Chalet for him way back then, right, Mom?" She didn't need her mother to answer, but something else about what she'd said didn't make sense either. "Never mind that, what do you mean, Maribeth really believed it? The house isn't haunted? That family, the Kellys, they didn't all die here?"

Both her parent shook their heads. "No, it's not haunted, and the Kellys didn't die here," her mother said. "Well, Mike Kelly did go over the cliff, but it didn't kill him, and the wife, what was her name?"

"Alexis," her father answered.

"Alexis did disappear, but their daughter never died. Well, not then, anyway. I mean, I don't know what happened to her afterwards, I don't think there's anybody still in town who does know, if anyone ever did."

That sounded confusing, but Ariel had long experience untangling her mother's run-on sentences. "So nobody actually died. Did the wife, Alexis, did she kidnap the daughter or something? Like a custody fight and it got ugly and horrible?"

"Something like that," her father said. "But that's another story, and we aren't even halfway through this one."

She did want to hear the rest of the tale of what had happened with Maribeth and the kiss. Not only did the diary not mention that, it was also silent on the aftermath.

"That's right, Mom. What did you do when you saw Maribeth kiss Dad?"

"I was very calm, and I pretended I didn't see anything, and I went home and forgot all about it and everything was back to normal the next morning." Her mother couldn't even make it halfway through that answer with a straight face. Her father didn't even need to say anything. "Fine," she said, pouring herself another glass of wine. "I was upset. Anybody would have been! So I went home and I stayed up all night trying to figure out a way to kill Maribeth and make it look like an accident. Are you happy now?"

"We did promise Ariel the whole truth, Sheryl," her father said. "Anyway, and this is another lesson for you, young lady, there's nothing wrong with feeling upset when something unpleasant happens, or even with fantasizing for a moment about avenging yourself upon someone who's done you wrong. As long as it is only a moment. Get your feelings out, and then calm down and think rationally about the situation and how to fix whatever is wrong. Without hurting anyone else in the process, ideally."

"Did you do that, Mom?"

"Kind of," her mother said. "I mean, I didn't actually hurt anybody…"

17.

SHERYL - THEN

There was a tiny part of Sheryl's mind that recognized she was ultimately responsible for what she'd seen outside the Firehouse Grille.

But it was only a tiny part, and it was massively outvoted by the rest of her mind, which was screaming for immediate retaliation.

At the moment, though, short of throwing either Maribeth or Jon - or both of them! - into traffic to be run over by a truck, there was nothing she could do. Anyway, throwing Maribeth in front of a truck would be far too merciful. How dare she kiss Jon! Not ten feet away from her! And how dare he let himself be kissed!

For maybe thirty seconds she just stood there, right outside the front door of the Grille, staring at the spot where it had happened. The exiting crowd had blocked her view of Jon and Maribeth, and she honestly couldn't tell if he'd seen her standing there or not. But Maribeth definitely had.

"Sheryl, come on. I'll walk you home." It was Vanessa.

"Absolutely not! Did you see what happened?"

Vanessa was holding her arm, pulling her away from the restaurant. "Yes, and so did everyone else, but there's nothing to be done about it now. Let's go, you live in the West Tower, right?"

She did indeed live in the West Tower of the Emerald Falls Condominiums, but she was in no state to direct her junior partner at the moment. She did allow herself to be led away, though. Vanessa was probably right; it wouldn't do to make a scene out here in front of dozens of people. Especially not when the person who most needed to see it had probably left already.

Sheryl didn't really notice where they were until they got to the lobby of her building; that horrible kiss was on infinite replay in the theater of her mind.

"What's your code?" She didn't answer; she still couldn't turn off the movie playing in her head, as much as she wanted to. "Never mind, your birthday is March 24th, let's try 0324."

Sheryl heard her voice speaking, but she had no idea where the words were coming from. She supposed there must be something like an autopilot deep in the farthest recesses of her brain. "0716. My mother's birthday."

"That's sweet," Vanessa said as the lock buzzed and she pulled the door open.

"I missed it two years ago, so I changed the code. That way I'd never forget it." There was the autopilot voice again. It did sound sort of like her normal voice, except with all the energy and emotion and life drained out of it.

Vanessa led her to the elevator, and up to the twenty-third floor, and down the hall to her apartment. Sheryl's keys were in her hand, although she couldn't remember fishing them out of her purse.

In they went. "Wow, this is actually nice," Vanessa said. Any other time, Sheryl would have been insulted by the way that had been phrased. But the horror movie to end all horror movies was still playing. "I like that vase by the window, and - ooh, that orchid is gorgeous."

The mention of the orchid cut through the endless visions of the kiss. "That bastard! How could he give me that and then - and then kiss - kiss that…"

Vanessa grabbed her before she could reach the vase. "I'm not going to let you smash it, Sheryl. You told me how much it cost, remember? I know you can't afford to throw money around like that. I see all the financial statements, remember?"

She said that with a smile, and Sheryl nearly laughed despite herself.

"You're right. He's not worth it."

Vanessa had maneuvered her onto the couch. "Yes he is, and you know it. And you also know he didn't kiss her. She kissed him, and she did it just to make you jealous."

"Well, mission accomplished." Maribeth might be loath-some well beyond the capacity of the English language to adequately express, but Sheryl had to admit the woman did have a flair for twisting the knife. "But how do you know he didn't kiss her back?"

"Because," Vanessa said, with exaggerated patience, "he loves you. God only knows why, but he does, and you know it, so get it out of your head that he did anything wrong."

She certainly hoped that was true. He acted like it was, most of the time, except when he completely lost his patience with her.

But maybe - just like the way she got so frustrated with him - it was actually a sign that he loved her even more than she dared hope. If he didn't have strong feelings for her, he wouldn't lose his patience, eventually he'd just walk away.

Except, if that was true, why didn't he just walk away from Maribeth? She would have to, she supposed, accept that he'd simply been surprised and unable to do anything but stand there and be kissed for a moment.

"If he didn't do anything wrong, then it's all on her. And I am not going to let her get away with it!"

Vanessa got up, went into the kitchen, returned a couple of minutes later with a pair of wineglasses. She handed one to Sheryl and took a sip from the other. "Not bad," she said. "A little sweet but not too bad." She downed the rest of the glass before going on. "Think about it, Sheryl. She *isn't* going to get away with it. You realize Will probably saw it, too. I don't picture him as the broad-minded type when it comes to his fiancée kissing other men."

That was true. Maribeth surely had a story already cooked up and ready to go for him, but he wasn't an idiot. Well, not that much of one. Not usually, anyway.

If Will had seen it, and if he was already disinterested in the family business - he wouldn't be playing in his band if he really wanted to be at Starwood Industries full time, right? - then it probably wouldn't be that hard to drive the wedge between him and Maribeth - and between him and the family company - even deeper. And she had a very good idea what might do it.

Sheryl began work on the new and improved plan first thing Thursday morning. She locked herself in her office and began dialing the phone. It took a dozen calls to find the place she was searching for, and an hourlong conversation with a woman who'd thoroughly creeped her out once she did find it. But she'd gotten what she wanted in the end.

Any time now, Will Starwood would receive a phone call from one Ms. Hilary Jackson, owner of a bar on Manhattan's Upper West Side. Ms. Jackson would offer him and Pay the Bill a regular monthly gig, starting this Sunday night. With any luck, Will would accept, and completely forget about the board meeting scheduled for nine o'clock the next morning.

Sheryl only knew about the bar from the girl who'd caused so much trouble during her and Jon's visit to Mallorca last Christmas. Jane Barnaby had been her name, and at one point during the week they'd been there, the girl had talked about a wine bar only a block or two from her sublet apartment off Central Park West, and how she'd occasionally go when they had a band - usually jazz - on Sunday nights.

Unfortunately, Jane hadn't mentioned - or Sheryl had forgotten - the actual name of the place, hence the dozen calls to discover that it was called In Vino Veritas. Which was appropriate, wasn't it? If all went well, Will would discover the truth there, that he had no business being engaged to Maribeth, or allowing her to control his shares of the family business.

Or, failing that, there was at least a decent chance he and the band would get drunk after the show, oversleep the next morning, and he'd completely miss the board meeting. That would satisfy Annalise Starwood, and ensure the continued survival of Mirage Cosmetics.

As plans went, it seemed close to foolproof. Really, what could go wrong?

18.

JON – THEN

Jon's father had been a high school chemistry teacher, and on the subject of sophomore year chem lab, he'd always said, "When you don't hear any more explosions, that's when it's time to worry about what's going on in there."

Jon had never understood that before, but almost forty-eight hours after what had happened outside the Firehouse Grille, he now knew exactly what his father meant.

He'd seen Sheryl, immediately after Maribeth had let him go, but before his brain had really, properly registered what had just happened. He realized in the space of a heartbeat that she'd seen the kiss, but then the crowd exiting the restaurant had gotten in the way before he could take a step towards her and try to explain. By the time the dust had settled, she was nowhere to be found.

To his surprise, there had been no angry message on his answering machine when he got home, no outraged knock on the door at three o'clock in the morning, no angry visit to his office the next day. There'd been nothing at all from her all until Thursday afternoon, and even then, it wasn't anything he'd expected. When his two-thirty appointment was finished, Monique handed him a note - Sheryl had called to ask how he was doing, and to wish him a good afternoon. And that was it.

Sheryl Jones was many things, but subtle was not one of them. Nor was patient. And yet that message was both. "She sounded like a normal person," Monique had said. "I wondered if maybe she was sick, but she didn't sound like she had a cold or anything."

Then, later that day, about an hour after he'd gotten home from work and just as he was getting ready to go into the kitchen and contemplate what he might have for dinner, the doorbell rang, and there she was, smiling, with a bag in her hands.

It was just a plain brown paper bag, but one whiff was all he needed to know from whence it had come. "Is that a chili cheeseburger from the Lighthouse Diner?"

"With a double order of French Fries," Sheryl had said. "I'll never understand how you can have such a fancy palate and still eat this stuff." She'd handed him the bag, and stepped back outside. "I can't stay," she'd explained. "But I wanted to treat you to a good - well, a meal you enjoy, anyway. So *bon appetit*, and I'll try to call you tomorrow. Good night, Jon."

The whole thing had left him at a complete loss. Nothing about Sheryl's behavior made sense.

It continued to not make sense today. She'd called the office again, right after lunch, and, again, she sounded calm and rational and entirely undisturbed about the fact that she'd watched her mortal enemy kiss him just two days ago. She hadn't said a word about the incident; she'd only asked if he had enjoyed dinner, and then apologized for forgetting that his annual physical was coming up soon. "I hope I didn't mess up your cholesterol. I know how Tabitha gets about that."

"I already had it, and I got a glowing report from her." He'd had a whole conversation with Sheryl about it at the time, and she'd demanded to see his blood test results.

"Oh, that's wonderful! I'm sure you told me and I forgot, I apologize." He couldn't think of the last time she'd apologized for anything unbidden. "That was terribly thoughtless of me."

Sheryl was behaving like - well, like a pod person. He could think of no better way to describe it. And since pod people weren't real, and real human beings did not completely change their entire personality overnight, there was only one conclusion to draw: Sheryl was plotting an epic vengeance against Maribeth, and possibly against himself as well, and her serene-to-the-point-of-insanity demeanor of the last two days was either an act to throw him off the scent, or a display of supreme self-satisfaction because the plan was proceeding, well, as planned.

He had to find out what was really going on with her.

Before he could set his mind to figuring out how, exactly, he might manage that, his phone rang. Monique announced the caller. "It's some woman named Cassie, she says she's a friend?"

"She is. Put her through please, Monique." Cassie had been there on that eventful week in Mallorca last December. The week had ended with Cassie's wedding, at which Sheryl had served as Matron of Honor.

"Jon?"

"Cassie, it's good to hear from you. Or should I call you Mrs. Barnaby now?"

"It's still Worthington. The lawyer said that changing my name on all the paperwork for the restaurant would cost ten grand, and my husband isn't that traditional."

She'd talked about the restaurant that she was head chef at - and, apparently, part-owner of? - during the trip. He and Sheryl had both discussed going there, but they'd never found the time.

"Ten thousand dollars is a lot of money," Jon agreed. "I assume married life is treating you well?"

"Very well," she said. "And that's why I'm calling. We've been meaning to have a get together at the restaurant ever since we got back, but you know how that goes."

He laughed. "The best laid plans of mice and men, and all that. But I presume you've set a date?"

She had indeed. "This Sunday, four o'clock. I hope you and Sheryl can join us."

A three hour trip down to Manhattan would give him plenty of time to talk to Sheryl uninterrupted, and get to the bottom of whatever it was she was planning. Besides, she had been Matron of Honor, she could hardly refuse to go. "We certainly will. Give me the address and we will be there."

He chatted with Cassie for another few minutes, then as soon as she was off the phone, he dialed Sheryl's office. She answered on the first ring.

"Hello?"

"Sheryl, it's Jon."

"Doc! I was just thinking of you."

Again the happy and serene tone of voice. It was positively disconcerting, but he put his misgivings aside and recapped his conversation with Cassie.

"Oh, that's perfect! Sunday afternoon is absolutely perfect! And I've got the perfect dress to wear. It'll be wonderful!"

He'd thought he would have to do some convincing, maybe even a little bit of guilting her into going, but she'd surprised him again. She was almost too eager to go. Why was Sunday afternoon so "perfect?" He fished a little for an answer but got nowhere; he'd just have to wait until they were on the train and then he'd pin her down on exactly what was going on.

***

They'd been on the Metro North train for more than an hour before Sheryl finally let something slip about her mysterious plans.

"It really was good timing that Cassie wanted to have her little party today."

"And why is that?"

"Well, I was going to keep it for a surprise, but what the heck," she said. "It turns out Will Starwood's band is playing in the city tonight. We should totally go."

Jon shook his head. It made perfect sense that she'd use Will and his band again. It had certainly gotten a reaction from Maribeth the first time. "'It turns out?' I never trust anything that someone tells me using the passive voice. What did you do, Sheryl?"

Now, finally, the reaction she'd been suppressing since Wednesday night came. It was like a dam breaking; the calm and serenity were swept away in an instant. Anger flashed in her eyes, and she nearly shouted her answer, causing the few heads in the train car to turn and stare at her. "I did what I had to do! That miserable, lying, conniving, cheating witch kissed you right in front of me! I couldn't let that go unpunished! If they still had duels, I would have been within my rights to call her out and shoot her at dawn! And you're the one she kissed, so you can't pretend you don't understand."

Disturbing as her words were - especially the part about duels - it was still a relief to hear them out loud. Once someone acknowledged their feelings, then there was a chance to talk about them, and ideally guide the person to a healthier way to handle them. So, in a way, this was progress.

"I do understand why you were upset, of course. And I apologize for - well, honestly there wasn't really anything I could have done in the moment, but I can imagine how upset you were, and I am sorry for that."

"You could have pushed her away. Or slapped her."

"I was too shocked to do anything. That's the God's honest truth." It was, too. "If I'd had any idea she was going to do something like that, I would have stopped her. Whatever our issues at the moment, there is no one else I want to kiss but you." Again, that was the absolute truth, and from the way her expression began to soften, she believed it. "But let us put all that aside. What does Will's band playing a gig in Manhattan have to do with Maribeth, or your efforts to do Annalise's bidding?" He realized what the answer was before he finished asking the question. "You hope he won't make it back in time for the board meeting tomorrow morning."

Now she smiled. It was a rather disconcerting, almost predatory smile. "No, I am going to make absolutely sure he doesn't make it back for the board meeting tomorrow morning. I'm going to help him and the band celebrate their first New York City gig and make sure he ends up with the worst hangover in the history of hangovers, and you're going to help me, aren't you?" The smile was softer suddenly, almost but not quite pleading. It took a lot of strength to resist that from her, and after an hour on the train, Jon simply didn't have it in him. Apparently, he was going to spend his Sunday night listening to a mediocre cover band and helping the bored and irresponsible heir to a major fortune get blind drunk. He supposed there were worse ways to spend an evening, although he couldn't think of any at the moment.

19.

ARIEL - NOW

"So I guess you got Will drunk and he missed his meeting?" Her mother had written about the party with the couple they'd met in Spain, but there'd been no entries for the whole next week after that

Her mother had the good grace to look embarrassed. "We certainly did." Her father looked uncomfortable at her use of "we" but he didn't correct her. "We did go to Cassie's party first, though. And that was really nice. You've been to her restaurant - remember, we went there when we took you to see *Mamma Mia* on Broadway for your sixteenth birthday?"

Ariel did remember. She'd loved it, her mother had been absolutely transported, to the point of singing along with nearly every song, and her father had sat through the whole show with a patient smile plastered on his face for three hours.

"That's her? Melissa's mom?" Melissa Barnaby was a year older than Ariel; they'd been fast friends at Theater Camp together for two straight years, back when she was in junior high school.

"That's her. Her and her husband, Joe. So we had a great time with them, then we went over to the Upper West Side, to this little wine bar on West 88th St. Honestly, it's kind of a blur after that, but I do remember waking up in my own bed the next morning." Ariel had only seen her mother drunk on a handful of occasions, but on those occasions, she had done a thorough job of it.

"Yes, because I made sure you got there, and I made you take three aspirin before you went to sleep so you wouldn't have the same hangover you gave to poor Will." Her father had a very self-satisfied glint in his eye.

"You didn't get drunk too, Dad?" She'd never seen him drunk, or even tipsy for that matter. Not even tonight, after a full bottle of wine and then some.

"I knew someone would have to remain sober and in control of his faculties," he said. "I suppose it comes with the territory. Nobody wants a psychiatrist who can't control his own behavior." He sighed, gestured towards the living room and the big wall-mounted TV. "Which is yet another reason that wretched *Fraiser* show is a slander against the good name of my entire profession. But I digress."

"Yes, you do, Doc," her mother said. "Anyway, Will missed his board meeting, and there were fireworks when he wasn't there in the family room at the Starwood mansion at nine o'clock Monday morning, let me tell you…"

20.

SHERYL - THEN

There was a sound. A loud, awful sound that was bypassing her ears and hammering straight into whatever part of her brain controlled her hearing. Jon would surely know what it was called; all Sheryl knew was that if it didn't stop her head would explode.

It couldn't be her alarm; that was set for 6:45 AM, and she could see that it was still dark out. There was no sunshine peeking in from behind the blinds, and hadn't the overly perky woman on Channel Twelve News said last night that sunrise was scheduled for around six o'clock this morning?

It wasn't the smoke detector; as loud as this sound was, that was even worse. It physically hurt her ears whenever it went off.

It was the phone. The phone was ringing, and it wasn't even six o'clock in the morning. Who on Earth could be calling at this hour?

The only thing she could think of was that, maybe, it was a call about Aunt Millie, who was in a nursing home in Phoenix, Arizona. If something had happened to her, Sheryl was on the list of people to contact. On the other hand, Sheryl was ten or twelve places down on that list, and, anyway, weren't they three hours behind out there in Arizona?

There was nothing for it. She would have to answer the phone if she wanted to know who was calling her at this ungodly hour.

"Sheryl?" It took her a moment to recognize the voice of her ex-husband.

"Brad? Brad Starwood? What are you doing up at this hour? And why are you waking *me* up?"

He didn't bother to answer. "Is my brother there?"

"No! Why would…" Her voice trailed off as it all came back to her. No wonder the phone had been so loud; red wine always gave her a bad morning after. Especially two or three bottles of it.

But if Brad Starwood was calling her to ask about Will's whereabouts, then it had all been worth it. The plan had succeeded beyond her wildest dreams.

"So he's not there? Are you sure?"

"I think I would know if your brother was in my bedroom. And as I'm sure you remember, I live in a one bedroom condo, so there's not much space here for him to be anywhere else."

Her headache was already fading; it must be the rush of endocrines or hemocytes or whatever the chemicals were called that flooded your brain when you were extremely happy. Brad would probably know; he was a doctor himself, after all. And now she thought about it, he sounded pretty pleased. A lot more pleased than somebody calling around before dawn in search of a sibling had any business being.

"I didn't think he'd be there, but I had to cover all the bases. His fiancée called me fifteen minutes ago, in a complete panic. She can't find him, can't reach him, apparently he dropped off the map yesterday."

Oh, this was just getting better and better! With any luck, Will would be passed out until noon and hungover for the rest of the day, and Maribeth would be tearing her professionally bleached hairs out one by one the whole time.

"Well, I can't imagine where he might be. But I'm sure he's fine. Will's a big boy, he can take care of himself."

"Why don't I believe that?" There was almost a teasing note in his voice. He was definitely enjoying this.

"I'm sure I couldn't say," she answered. "But it's the truth. I don't know where he is." Technically, that *was* true. She didn't know which room of the St. Ives Hotel on 93rd and Madison Will was currently sleeping in, or exactly where in that room he had finally collapsed.

"I'm sure you know there's a board meeting today. Nine o'clock sharp."

"Really?" It occurred to Sheryl that this much fun, this early in the morning, probably ought to be illegal.

"Really. And, wouldn't you know it, I've got a surgery scheduled for eight-thirty this morning, so I don't see how I can be there myself."

He wasn't - he didn't mean - things couldn't be working out this perfectly, could they? "That's inconvenient for the family. What will they do without you or Will there?"

She realized she'd slipped up, but Brad didn't seem to notice, or maybe he was deliberately letting it pass. "Well, if both of us were absent, and there were no instructions on how our shares should be voted, I suppose father would have to reschedule the meeting. And you know how upset he gets when he has to do that."

Noah Starwood did have quite the temper. She'd been witness to it a few times, and the target once or twice. "It sounds like you have something in mind, Brad."

He did. "I presume you can be at the mansion at nine o'clock sharp?"

Yes, he was going to do it. "Not that I'm not unbelievably grateful, Brad, because I am. I mean, I can't even tell you, this is like my birthday and Christmas and Valentine's Day all wrapped up in one. But I have to ask, why?"

He didn't quite laugh. "Two reasons. First of all, I know it was three years ago, and you never complained, but you didn't really get a fair deal in the divorce, and I figure I owe you one. Second, I don't like Maribeth Peale any more than you do, and just imagining her face when you walk into the family room this morning is the best laugh I've had in ages."

Sheryl spent a good half hour staring at herself in the mirror. She tried on four different suits, seven pairs of earrings and a dozen necklaces before she finally decided that she had the perfect look for the board meeting.

Her makeup took another half hour. No detail was too small; everything had to be just right.

The drive to the Starwood mansion, normally a trip of ten minutes, fifteen at the worst, took forty minutes, because the speedometer never inched above twenty miles an hour. Sheryl had no intention of getting a ticket, or, God forbid, getting into a fender-bender on the way.

She made it there without incident, unless you counted the three times she was honked at for driving so slowly, and made the right turn into the huge horseshoe-shaped driveway. She passed Maribeth's black Audi, and the hunter green Jaguar that belonged to one of the Starwood grandsons. She could never recall which one owned the Jag, and which one had gotten a BMW for his eighteenth birthday.

Her cherry red Miata really didn't look terribly out of place in comparison. Of course, that was only because Noah Starwood's prized Rolls Royce Silver Phantom was hidden away in the garage, protected from the elements, as well as grease stains, fingerprints, covetous looks, or anything else that might dare to besmirch it. Next to that car, almost anything would look like a piece of junk.

There was no need to lock the Miata; nobody in their right mind would try to steal a car out of the Starwood driveway. Sheryl just left it there and walked the few steps up to the front door, which opened without her having to ring the bell.

"Joseph! It's nice to see you. You're efficient as ever." Joseph had been here three years ago during her brief marriage to Brad Starwood. He hadn't changed a bit; it even looked like the same suit he'd worn then. And upon closer inspection, it was. She could see the tiny spot on the shoulder that had had to be repaired after that incident with the candles in the main dining room.

"Ms. Jones, it's good to see you as well." She had never quite gotten used to the fact that Joseph didn't have a British accent. It was silly, but after a lifetime watching movies where the butler was always English, she couldn't help but expect Joseph to speak that way, no matter how often she reminded herself he was as American as she was. "Bradley informed me you would be coming. I haven't told the rest of the family. I hope you'll forgive me. I get so little amusement these days." That was surely true; working for the Starwoods had to be challenging at the best of times.

He ushered her into the house. Nothing had changed in the entry hall; the portrait of Noah's father still hung on one wall, and a stone statue of a bulldog stood guard just inside the door. She petted good old Rocky before Joseph led her into the living room.

This room did look a little different than the last time she'd seen it. A black leather sofa had replaced the brown leather one that used to face the fireplace. And a lot of the knickknacks and curios had been switched out. Not that knickknacks or curios was an adequate description; some of the items were worth more than her car, and she suspected a couple of them were worth more than her condo. You could stock a small museum - or a large one, for that matter - with everything the Starwoods owned.

"Everyone is already here for the meeting, excepting of course Bradley. Shall I show you in?"

It was five minutes to nine, but there was no point waiting. She'd only get nervous if she did, and this was no time for nerves. "Yes, please. I can't wait to see their faces."

Joseph gave her the briefest of grins and led her down the back hallway and to the family room. He knocked at the closed door - Sheryl had been surprised, the first time she visited, that it wasn't soundproofed.

From inside, she heard the gruff voice of Noah Starwood. "Is that my son? Come in and let's get this wretched business started already."

Joseph opened the door, and announced her. "Ms. Sheryl Jones." She heard a babble of voices, and Maribeth's shout of "What the hell!" cutting through them.

"Ms. Sheryl Jones," he repeated, and then he reached into his inside jacket pocket and pulled out an envelope. "And a letter from Bradley appointing Ms. Jones as his proxy for today's meeting."

The butler walked into the room and handed the letter to old Noah. Noah Starwood was a big man, easily six foot two, and still reasonably well-muscled. Sheryl supposed that having two doctors in the family would make it easier to stay in good shape.

Noah, and everyone else in the room – excepting Maribeth – were sitting in exactly the same places they'd been in the last time Sheryl had attended a Starwood Industries board meeting, three years ago.

Noah himself sat on a plush loveseat, with his wife, Eleanor. Unlike the butler, she did have something close to a British accent, which had always struck Sheryl as odd, considering that she'd spent her whole life here in Emerald Falls. She wore a dress that wouldn't have been out of place in an old movie, but then again, almost everything about her felt like that.

Next to them, in the most comfortable chair in the room - Sheryl had made a study of it during her six weeks of marriage - was her predecessor and successor as Brad's wife, Dr. Tabitha Starwood. Behind her, in a huge leather swivel chair was Annalise.

The only thing different than three years ago was Maribeth. She stood all by herself, in the far corner of the room, pointedly looking away from Sheryl. She was wearing exactly the same coral Chanel suit as Sheryl herself. Of course she was.

Noah examined the letter. "My son wrote this, Joseph?"

"In my presence, Mr. Starwood."

Noah's face, which was already close to red, was beginning to edge towards purple. "And he didn't have the courtesy to inform his family beforehand?"

Joseph's face was perfectly straight; Sheryl thought he'd be hell to play against at the poker table. "I cannot read Bradley's mind, sir. All I can tell you is what I've said. He wrote the letter in my presence, sealed it in the envelope and told me to expect Ms. Jones. It's not my place to question members of the family."

Noah started to answer, but a sharp glance from Tabitha stopped him in his tracks. Sheryl could guess what she was thinking: if he asked Joseph to rat out Brad, then the butler might also rat out Noah himself to Tabitha and her husband. He might tell them about the late-afternoon cigars and the cream sauces Noah smuggled into the house in defiance of their dietary orders.

He sighed and said, "Well, what's done is done, and everything seems to be in order. At least one of my sons, obnoxious as it was to do it by letter, had the decency to let us know of his whereabouts." He glanced at the butler. "Joseph, you may go about your duties, and Sheryl, sit yourself down so we can get this over with."

She did as she was told, settling into the other loveseat. She could feel Maribeth glaring at her, trying to bore a hole in the back of her head through sheer force of will.

"We can't start," Maribeth said after a moment or two, trying vainly to keep her voice under control. "Will isn't here. We don't have the full board!"

"We don't need the full board, Maribeth," Annalise said. The self-satisfaction in her tone was a marvel to behold. "Perhaps you've never studied the bylaws. Seventy-five percent of the voting members must be present to transact business. Five out of seven members only makes up seventy-one percent, but Sheryl's arrival puts us over the top." The smile she directed at Maribeth was cold enough to cause frostbite. "I have a calculator handy if you'd like to double-check the figures for yourself."

It was undeniably impressive watching Annalise put Maribeth in her place. Still, Sheryl couldn't help but feel a twinge of sympathy for her rival, having been on the receiving end of Annalise's attentions just a few days ago herself. Thankfully, though, after this meeting, she'd never need to worry about that again.

21.

JON - THEN

His phone was ringing for the third time. Monique knew he was in a session, she knew not to disturb him, especially with poor Bella Travers, who'd already been rescheduled twice last week. If she felt something was important enough to try three times to reach him despite that, it must be urgent.

"Yes, Monique?"

She was apologetic. "Forgive me, Doctor Hardy, but I've got a woman on the line who says she's got a bottle of pills and she's going to take them all unless you talk to her right now."

In his experience, someone who made a call like that had no intention of actually going through with their threat; they were generally seeking attention. People who really wanted to kill themselves usually just went ahead and did it. But

Monique wasn't to know that; she was right to interrupt him. "Go ahead and put her through. And thank you for keeping at it. That's excellent work." Before the call clicked through, he apologized to Bella. "Please excuse me. It seems I've got an emergency call on the line."

The moment the call was transferred, and he heard who was on the other end of the line, he knew it was no emergency. "Jon, I know you're with a patient and I don't care. I've only got two minutes, and you need to listen to me if you want to continue working at the hospital."

It was Maribeth Peale, and she was in a state that he'd never observed her in before. He heard anger, icy determination and barely-controlled panic, mixed together with a sharp note of self-pity.

Despite the interruption, and the insult and the worrying combination of emotions, he was more curious than anything else. What could have happened to drive Maribeth to this state? "I am with a patient, and I don't respond to threats." He caught himself before saying her name; Bella had no need to know to whom he was speaking. "But if you'd like to calm down and call back in twenty minutes, I'll clear my next appointment and we can talk about whatever is going on."

There was a sound that he couldn't identify, somewhere between a growl and a laugh. "I don't have twenty minutes. And if you want to keep your job, you don't, either. You call your girlfriend right now, right this minute, and I don't care what you say, but you get her to change her vote or you'll be the subject of an emergency hospital board meeting tomorrow morning."

The Starwood board meeting! Of course, that had to be it. Today was Monday, it was a quarter after nine, but what on Earth did she mean about Sheryl having a vote? Why would Sheryl even be at that meeting?

"I don't think I quite understand. What vote?"

Maribeth's voice was even more impatient now. "Don't play dumb, Jon. I don't know how she managed it, but your girlfriend is here, and she's the deciding vote, and if my division gets shut down because of her, I swear to you I won't just get you fired from the hospital, I'll see to it that you lose your license to practice anywhere. Call her right now, or I'll do it."

There was a click, and Maribeth was gone, but he couldn't in good conscience continue the session. He needed time to process what had just been said. "Bella, I apologize, but I need to deal with this crisis immediately. I'll have Monique reschedule you - I'll move appointments around for your convenience, all right?"

A moment later, he was alone, the door locked, and he could think more clearly. Maribeth probably couldn't get him fired, but as a board member, she could make life complicated for him. And there were definitely things in his past, both recent and farther back, that, even though they weren't actual ethical violations, could be made to look bad.

At a minimum, he could try Sheryl's cell phone. She might answer, and then he could hear her side of things and make a more informed decision. But, naturally, it went straight to voicemail.

He could call the Starwood mansion and try to reach her that way. But perhaps there was a way to stop the proceedings over there without speaking to Sheryl at all. Strictly speaking, this *would* be an ethical violation, but it also seemed to be the least bad choice.

Two minutes later, Monique knocked on the door, and he beckoned her in. "I did it, Doctor Hardy. But would you mind telling me why I sent that message to Dr. Starwood's beeper?"

He didn't quite laugh. "It was the lesser of several evils. And when she comes here to read you the riot act for it, you will tell her that you were trying to send a message to my new beeper as a test, using the instructions I gave you, and I will agree that the blame is entirely mine."

"I've been here long enough to know better than to ask stupid questions, but I have to know why. Because that was screwy even for this hospital." Monique never questioned anything he asked of her - not that he usually asked anything very far out of the ordinary - but he could hardly blame her for being curious.

"Honestly, I don't really know myself. I was just trying to defuse a situation and buy some time for cooler heads to prevail." Not that they probably would, but what else could he have done?

―――――――

Dr. Tabitha Starwood's head was far from cool when she arrived at his office an hour later. "What the hell was that all about, Jon? Your receptionist gave me some cockamamie story about testing out your beeper, but we both know that's nonsense."

He closed the door and locked it, then went to his desk and picked up the phone. "Monique, can you reschedule my ten-thirty please? Thank you." He put the phone down, straightened the papers on the desk, took a deep, calming breath and faced Tabitha.

Not for the first time, he wondered how the same man could have married both Tabitha and – however briefly – Sheryl. It was difficult to imagine how they could both be any one man's type. Tabitha was a good six inches shorter than Sheryl, and at least ten years older. And in terms of temperament, they couldn't be more different.

"You were about to answer me, Jon?"

"Yes, Tabitha." There was no point lying to her. She knew he was dating - or whatever you could call it - Sheryl, and she knew about Sheryl's feud with Maribeth. "I had to do something to stop the board meeting. I only hope I did it in time."

"You did." She allowed herself a small smile. "Annalise was beside herself, but she could hardly complain about me leaving for a medical emergency, could she?" The smile disappeared. "Maribeth called you, didn't she? When she excused herself to the bathroom. She called you and, let me guess, she threatened to bring you up in front of the hospital board."

He was surprised, but only for an instant. It wasn't difficult to puzzle out, really. What else could Maribeth have said to push him into action like that? "She did. But, truthfully, I wasn't worried about that. I simply wanted to deescalate the situation."

"Do no harm?"

"Something like that," he said. "Since you're here, perhaps you can enlighten me. How did Sheryl find herself at your family's board meeting?"

Tabitha shook her head. "You can thank my husband for that. He rearranged his schedule so he'd be in surgery this morning, and he gave Sheryl his proxy for the meeting. His idea of a joke, I suppose."

She seemed surprisingly unbothered by that, considering that Sheryl had briefly been married to her husband. In fact, she seemed less bothered than he felt, hearing the news. Did Sheryl still have feelings for Brad, or he for her? "And you're okay with that?"

She was. "If I didn't believe he got her thoroughly out of his system, I wouldn't have married him again. Besides, I work with an old ex myself, so if he doesn't complain about that, I can hardly say anything about him talking to Sheryl every once in a while."

Maybe she should be the psychiatrist; she had a pretty solid handle on her feelings, and a refreshingly mature view on relationships. "When you put it that way, I can't disagree." He was curious, though, which other doctor on staff – it had to be a doctor, didn't it? – was her ex. But that was a question for another time.

"Good," she replied. "Besides, seeing Maribeth's face when she walked into the room was a treat."

The woman certainly didn't have a lot of friends, did she? "So you don't get along with her?"

Now she laughed. "The only people in the family who do like her are Will, because she's sleeping with him, and my father-in-law, because he admires her ruthlessness."

Maribeth had always been civil enough with him - the incident last week excepted - but he could see how she would rub people the wrong way. "How did your brother-in-law end up with her?"

"Have you *met* Will?" She laughed. "He's the nicest one in the family, but he's got all the good judgment God gave your average squirrel." And apparently even less survival instinct than one, considering how angry Maribeth had been on the phone.

Jon realized that the phone hadn't rung the whole time Tabitha had been here. It was difficult to believe that Sheryl hadn't tried to call him in the aftermath of the board meeting breaking up early. Monique must have taken it upon herself to put Sheryl off. She deserved a raise.

***

Tabitha left just ahead of Jon's eleven-thirty appointment. Monique ushered his patient in, commenting as she did that "Your girlfriend called a dozen times. You don't pay me enough to put up with her." Well, it was good that they agreed, he supposed.

It was not the most productive therapy session he'd ever conducted, but, fortunately, Maurice Webber didn't seem to catch on. When Maurice's fifty minutes were up, he sent the man on his way and called Sheryl's cell phone. Which, for once, she actually answered.

"Doc? Are you finally done with all the patients? I need to talk to you!"

"Good morning to you, too, Sheryl, and I hope you're having a pleasant day so far." He sighed deeply. "I am free for the next hour, yes, if you can come to the hospital."

She barely let him finish the sentence. "I'm in the hospital cafeteria. Come on down here and buy me lunch. It's the least you can do after what you did today."

He sighed again, cursed himself for not having better sense, and headed down to the cafeteria. As promised, Sheryl was there, at a two-seater table near the big window looking south out at Galley St. and the woods beyond it.

"I would have waited in your waiting room," she said by way of greeting, "but your receptionist was giving me the ugliest looks, and I just couldn't stand it anymore so I came down here. But you have more to answer for than her, Dr. Hardy. What on Earth possessed you to call Tabitha Starwood away from the meeting, before we could vote to kill off Maribeth's division?"

She had to already know. Tabitha had figured it out, and whatever their difference in education, Sheryl was at least her equal in cunning. "Why are you asking a question you already know the answer to?"

She looked chastened, but only for a moment. "Because I want to know why you listened to a word that lying, conniving witch said!" Even before she finished speaking, though, he saw realization dawn in her eyes. "She didn't! She wouldn't! Even for her, that would be - even I wouldn't stoop that low!"

"She did."

Sheryl leaned back in her chair, holding on to the table as if to steady herself. "She really threatened to get you fired? But - but you have such a good record here, she could never convince the board to do it."

Probably not; he'd come to the same conclusion himself. "No. But an animal is at its most dangerous when it feels cornered. I know you watch the Nature Channel when you can't sleep late at night and there's nothing else on, so you know what I'm talking about. And, after all, we are all animals, aren't we?"

"Speak for yourself!" He felt it the better part of valor not to point out her leopard-print handbag, or that the color of her nail polish was called "Jungle Red."

"Putting biology aside, as I'm sure you know, Tabitha paid me a visit. And she told me that the next Starwood board meeting won't be for another week."

She just about growled at that. "Stupid bylaws! Annalise tried to push things through after Tabitha left, but Maribeth must have studied the rules because she got Noah to end the meeting, and according to the rules, every meeting has to be announced seven days in advance, so they can't have another one until next Monday. Which means..."

He finished for her. "Which means you're still not off the hook with Annalise. Or Maribeth. And since I intervened, neither am I."

22.

ARIEL - NOW

They'd retreated to the living room, and her father had a crackling fire going in the fireplace. Ariel supposed it was fitting to continue the tale by fireside.

"I can't believe Maribeth actually threatened to fire you from the hospital, Dad. That's crazy!"

He wagged a finger at her. "You know how I feel about that word, Ariel. But I agree, she was not acting entirely rationally during that whole affair."

It felt disloyal to even think it, but her mother hadn't exactly been on her best behavior either, by her own admission. "Mom? You never said in the diary. Why was Maribeth going after your company in the first place? The whole story started with her trying to get your magazine ads cancelled, but that wasn't really what started it." It wasn't a question.

Her father nodded in agreement. "You never told me what set Maribeth off either, Sheryl."

Her mother shrugged. "I won a client away from her. She was starting up a fashion division at Starwood, this was a couple of months before we met, Jon." Ariel didn't need to hear any more; she could see exactly what had happened next. Her mother would have gotten wind of a brand new competitor - except it didn't actually make sense, did it? Fashion and cosmetics weren't really competitors.

"How would a fashion company compete with Mirage?"

"Normally it wouldn't," she agreed. "But I was over at the Firehouse Grille one night, and I got to talking to Will Starwood, and he went on about how his fiancée talked Noah into letting her run a fashion division, but what she really wanted was to make it a whole lifestyle thing. You know, beauty products, accessories, everything. And I knew that she'd be coming after me, so, well, I decided to strike first." She laughed. "Like it says in the Bible, do unto others before they do unto you."

"That's not what it says in the Bible, Mom." On the other hand, Mirage Cosmetics had been her mother's baby, long before Ariel herself had been a gleam in anyone's eye. She could hardly blame her mother for being overprotective.

"I admit I never paid as much attention in Sunday School as I should have. But it all worked out in the end. And believe it or not, you can thank your Uncle Robert for that."

Uncle Robert? Her father's estranged - and that was a polite word for it - older brother? He called once a year, on Christmas morning, and the last time Ariel had seen him was six years ago. Her father never talked about him.

"Yes," her father said. He was making the same face he used to make when poor Sigmund threw up and he had to clean it up. "Robert picked the day of the board meeting to breeze into town and darken my doorstep. But that wasn't the first stop he made..."

23.

SHERYL - THEN

She was glad to see the back of the hospital cafeteria. The food was awful, and the whole place smelled of Lysol. She supposed that, were she a patient, she'd appreciate the attention to cleanliness, but as a visitor it only upset her stomach. Which needed nothing more to upset it after Maribeth had been allowed to escape from the board meeting with her division still intact.

Jon had done nothing to set her mind, or stomach, at ease. She couldn't really blame him for doing what he'd done. In his place, she would have done the same. Except, if she were being honest, she probably wouldn't have had the presence of mind to call Tabitha away with the excuse of a medical emergency.

That had been inspired thinking, she had to admit. But a lot more inspired thinking would be needed to deal with both Annalise and Maribeth before the next board meeting.

She decided to head back to her apartment. The office would get along just fine without her for an afternoon, and she could use some time to think in the peace and quiet of her living room.

It was not to be. Halfway up Third St., just past Bailey's Books and News, she saw Jon again. Except that made no sense. She'd left him at the hospital. He had a full schedule this afternoon, and, anyway, how could he have passed her on the sidewalk without her noticing? And since when did he wear a leather jacket?

But it was unmistakably him. "Doc?"

He turned to see who had called out to him, and she saw she was mistaken. The man looking back at her was not Jon, but he was a close facsimile. He had the same eyes, the same cheekbones, the same strong chin, the same ridiculously good hair. He even walked the same way.

"Do I know you?" The voice was almost the same, too. Not quite identical, but close enough. She knew Jon had a brother; he'd mentioned the fact a couple of times, but Sheryl didn't know the man's name, where he lived, or anything else about him.

"If you're who I think you might be, we've got somebody in common."

The man didn't exactly sneer, but that was the closest Sheryl could get to describing his expression. "The great Dr. Hardy, licensed psychiatrist?"

Sheryl felt compelled to defend her - well, whatever it was he was to her at the moment. "I don't think he'd say it like that, but, you know what, he is pretty great. And if you're his brother, you ought to count your lucky stars to have some-body like him for your brother."

OK, now he was definitely sneering. "Well, he always did have a way with women. I guess all that psychology is good for something. But have you ever asked yourself why he never talks about his beloved sibling?"

"How did you know that?" Sheryl knew as soon as the words were out of mouth that she shouldn't have spoken them. But what was done was done. And of course he had an answer at the ready.

"I've known him a lot longer than you have, darling." She didn't blame Jon one bit for not talking about him, if this was how he introduced himself to a complete stranger. "I could tell you a few things, if you'd join me at that coffee shop I passed down the street."

"The Koffee Hut?" Sheryl's first thought was to refuse, for several very good reasons. But maybe that was shortsighted. It couldn't hurt to hear what Jon's brother had to say. Even if he did nothing but lie about and slander Jon, he might inad-vertently reveal truths in the way he spoke, his body language.

Besides, Krista Walker would see him, and that could only be a good thing. Either she'd be attracted to Jon's brother, and start mooning over him instead of Jon; or she'd be repulsed by him, and some of that repulsion might carry over to her view of Jon and she'd stop mooning over him anyway. Either way, Krista and her mooning would cease to be a problem.

"I've got a few minutes free, why not?"

Unfortunately, Sheryl hadn't counted on Krista actually sitting down at their table, insinuating herself into their conversation and just making an all-around pest of herself. It didn't help that she brought Sheryl a cup of that horrible lavender-flavored dishwater she'd served last time. All in all, it was a depressing and wasted half-hour, in which she learned nothing except that Jon's brother bitterly resented him, and supposedly had some purpose in town entirely unrelated to Jon.

"I must be going," he said at two o'clock. "I have errands to see to. By the way, since you never did bother to ask, my name is Robert. Not Bob, not Robbie, but Robert. I'd appreciate it if you remembered that."

He stalked out of the Koffee Hut, and, for once, Sheryl and Krista agreed wholeheartedly on something. "Who the hell does that guy think he is?" They said it in unison about a second after the front door closed behind him, and then neither of them could help collapsing into laughter at the absurdity of what had just happened.

Robert Hardy was not the only surprise of the afternoon for Sheryl. When she unlocked the door to her apartment and stepped inside, she saw that it was not unoccupied.

Annalise Starwood was sitting - no, lounging! - on her sofa. Her $9,000 imported French sofa with hand-sewn upholstery, and Annalise was lounging on it, with her feet up on the armrest.

"I expected you an hour ago, Sheryl. You're not avoiding me, are you?"

There was no point asking how Annalise had gotten in. She could easily have picked the lock. Or bribed one of the maintenance men. Or, hell, maybe she'd turned into a bat, flown in through the bedroom window and changed back into human form again. Sheryl wouldn't honestly be surprised to discover the woman had access to demonic powers.

"Not that it's any of your business, but I stopped for some coffee on the way home."

Annalise gave her the Jaws smile. "If I were you, I'd have gotten something a little stronger. A little liquid courage would not go amiss, under the circumstances. You still have a job to do for me."

Her survival instinct kicked in, and discarded the first several responses that came to mind. "I do?" was what she finally said, in as innocent a tone as she could manage.

Now the smile was predatory enough to frighten poor Jaws himself. "Sheryl, please don't play dumb. It doesn't suit you." It was undeniably a compliment, but Sheryl felt she'd been insulted all the same. "You may not have the IQ of your friend the psychiatrist, but you are no idiot. Our agreement was that you would ensure Maribeth's shares voted as I wish." Now her expression softened fractionally. "I'll grant that your plan was inspired. And I will admit that I should have thought to lock the doors to the family room once the meeting began. But what's done is done, and we are still where we were. There will be another meeting a week from today, and I very much doubt that even my brother will fall for the same trick twice."

Sheryl doubted it, too. But she could see nothing else to do about Maribeth's shares, short of kidnapping the woman and holding her hostage until after the meeting. She was fairly sure Annalise would have no problem with that strategy, but while it was fun to think about, it wasn't a realistic option.

The battle lines had been clear in the meeting: Annalise, Tabitha and Brad all wanted to eliminate Maribeth's division. But together, they only controlled forty-nine and a half percent of the company stock.

Maribeth and Will obviously wanted to keep it in business, and Noah Starwood was siding with them, along with his wife, who always voted her shares in lockstep with Noah. And Noah held the extra half a percent which ensured that he only ever needed one of his children or children-in-law to side with him to win on any issue.

"What about your mother? Couldn't you get her on your side? Then it wouldn't matter what Maribeth did."

Annalise didn't laugh, but only because her glare made it clear that Sheryl's words were too stupid to even merit being laughed at. "My mother has never voted against my father. Not in my lifetime, at any rate."

Sheryl hadn't known that, but it did make sense. Eleanor Starwood was a strong woman, but to Sheryl's knowledge, she always deferred to her husband on matters of business. Even so, there had to be some way to drive a wedge between them.

She had a thought then, but she didn't dare speak it out loud. Annalise would either consider it an unforgiveable idea and destroy Sheryl's life in retaliation for even contemplating it; or, and she wasn't sure if this was worse, Annalise would deem it a great idea and order Sheryl to begin working on it immediately.

Better to just toss it in her mental trash can right now and move on. "If we can't get your mother to vote with you, is there any way to turn Noah against Maribeth?"

Annalise didn't quite scoff. "I don't see how. He likes Maribeth better than Will, not that I can blame him for that. She'd have to do something so offensive…"

Inspiration struck again, and this time it was something she wouldn't hate herself for. She blurted her thought out before Annalise could finish speaking.

"The Rolls!" Annalise just stared at her. Sheryl wasn't sure whether the surprise on Annalise's face was due to confusion over what she meant, or from shock that Sheryl had dared to interrupt her. It didn't matter. "His car. The Rolls Royce. If she messed it up, dented it, whatever, he'd go ballistic."

Noah's Rolls Royce was kept in a separate garage away from all the other cars the Starwoods owned, a garage which was temperature and humidity controlled, and more relevant at the moment, a garage was which kept locked at all times. Only Noah held the key; not even Joseph was allowed in the garage.

"That's true," Annalise agreed. At least she appeared to be considering the idea. "But he keeps it guarded tighter than Fort Knox. And Maribeth knows how he feels about the car. She got the same lecture you did when Bradley brought you home after he made the mistake of marrying you."

Sheryl let that pass. "Will knows all that, but I bet we could talk him into taking it for a joyride. And, anyway, locks can be picked." Not that she'd ever tried to do it, but how hard could it be?

Annalise approved. "That's a surprisingly good idea, actually. There's only one flaw. You keep saying 'we' but this is *your* job, Sheryl. I can let you know when my father is not in residence at the mansion, but that will be the extent of my involvement in this affair. I trust that you understand?"

Sheryl understood all too clearly.

24.

JON - THEN

"What are you staring at? Did I spill coffee on my tie?" After his three-thirty appointment had left, Jon decided to take a walk outside, to enjoy a few minutes of spring air and blooming flowers. What he got, though, was confused stares from several of his coworkers as he walked through the hospital lobby. After the fourth one, he grabbed Bob McConnell's arm and put the question to him.

"I'm looking at a man who can be in two places at once. I just ran over to Bailey's Books and News and I could swear I saw you browsing the magazines there." Bob considered his words, looked Jon up and down. "Except I don't think I've ever seen you wearing a leather jacket. Or anything other than dress shoes."

It was a measure of how much self-control he possessed that Jon didn't curse out loud. "Robert. What is he doing here?"

"I work here. You sure you're all right, Jon?"

Bob. Robert. It would be funny, if it were anyone but his thoughtless, dishonest excuse for a brother. "Not you. Him. My brother. Robert Hardy."

Bob laughed. "I get it now. But I didn't know you had a brother."

"Would that I could say the same. If he's here in town, it's to cause me grief. That's the one thing in this life he truly excels at."

Even that was understating things. Robert had gotten him suspended for a week in high school, and it was only their father's pleading that had allowed him to walk with the rest of his graduating class. Then he'd nearly gotten him expelled from college, blown up his relationships with two different girlfriends and torpedoed a third before she'd ever properly become his girlfriend, and come close to getting him deported from Austria a week before his dissertation defense.

"I guess it's like they say," Bob said, still smiling. "You can choose your friends, but you can't choose your family." He could smile; Robert Hardy wasn't here to ruin *his* life.

This was one of those times - they were infrequent, but he had to admit that they did happen on occasion - when he wished he had Sheryl's imagination, her gift for coming up with schemes to deal with people who had wronged her.

Unfortunately, he was unable to reach her on her cell phone, or at her office. But that was fine. She had to go home eventually.

Rather than call her, Jon decided to go straight to her apartment after his last appointment of the day. She had shown up unannounced at his office - and his home - often enough. Surely she wouldn't begrudge him turning the tables on her.

He remembered the code to the front door and went straight up to the twenty-third floor. When he rang the doorbell, she responded immediately. She shouted at him through the door. "Wow, you guys are fast! Let me just put some clothes on - never mind, forget you heard that!"

His heart began to race at those words. But he had to remind himself, this was - well, not business, exactly, but definitely not a personal call. A war council, maybe? Except, she wasn't expecting hi.

Worse, she *was* expecting somebody else. Which "guys" had she invited to her home?

The door opened a couple of minutes later, and Sheryl, wearing a red silk robe that showed off every single one of her curves to maximum effect, looked at him with - he'd never seen this in her eyes before - total, crestfallen disappointment.

"You're not the guy from the locksmith place!"

No, he wasn't. But that answered the question of who she'd been waiting for. "Why do you need a locksmith?"

She appeared not to hear his words. "They said they'd have a guy over here by eight o'clock, and at first I thought, no, they're just saying that, but then the bell rang, and I got my hopes up, and instead it's just you."

"It's good to see you too, Sheryl. Again I ask, why do you need a locksmith? Your door seems to be in perfectly good order." He'd heard the lock turn when she let him in; it didn't sound broken.

"You may as well come in and wait with me," she said, sighing. "Not that it'll probably do any good even if they do come tonight. Or tomorrow. I doubt they've got a lock that will keep Annalise out when she wants in."

Sheryl plopped herself down on the sofa. Jon sat next to her. "Annalise was here?"

She rolled her eyes. "Give the man a cigar. There's that keen insight into the human mind. Yes, Annalise was here! She was waiting for me, in my home, on my imported $9,000 sofa that I saved up my pennies for six months to buy!"

Jon very much doubted that any actual pennies were involved, but it seemed best not to say so. Instead, he pasted the closest thing he could manage to a smile on his face and asked her to tell him all about it.

Half an hour and several rants later, he had the full story. He couldn't honestly blame her for being upset; coming home to find Annalise Starwood sitting on one's couch was not a pleasant prospect at the best of times.

"Oh, and to top it all off, it was a crummy day even before I came home. Did you know you have a brother?"

What? Where the hell that that comment come from? Why would she possibly mention his brother now, when she'd never met him, and he never talked about him?

"Yes, I did know that." The words came out flat, almost emotionless. His brain was too preoccupied in processing what she'd said to come up with anything more intelligent.

He must have looked even more lost than he felt, because the near-manic look that had been in her eyes for the last half-hour vanished between one blink and the next, and now she was staring back at him with concern. And something more, that he dared not give a name to. "Well, that was stupid, of course you know you have a brother. But did you know he's here in town?" She reached out, took both his hands in hers. "No, you didn't, did you? You had no idea. But I do, and I understand why you're so upset."

She must have run into him. That was the only logical explanation. "Actually, I did know. I found out a couple of hours ago. Bob McConnell ran into him by the bookstore and mistook him for me. In certain lights, we do look rather similar to one another." He squeezed her hands. Her touch was helping, there was no doubt about that. "He's why I came over. I need your help dealing with him."

She squeezed his hands back. She could go right on doing that. "I don't think you need my help. What you need is a pest control guy. Or maybe an exorcist. He's a real piece of work." She paused for a moment, smiled the embarrassed smile that appeared whenever she realized she'd said something horribly rude when she hadn't actually intended to. "No offense."

"None taken." He let go of her hands and put an arm around her, pulled her close. "Believe me, there's nothing you could say about Robert that would offend me. 'Piece of work' is pretty mild."

She nodded. "Yeah, it is. But I'm still sorry. Most people don't like anyone else insulting their family, even the family they can't stand."

He'd observed that often enough in his practice. "Normally, you'd be right. But, first of all, you're not simply 'anyone else' and second, I doubt even you know any insult bad enough to offend me where my brother is concerned."

"You're about to tell me the whole story about him, aren't you." It wasn't a question, and she didn't wait for an answer. "That's fine, this is a crisis, and your crisis trumps mine for the moment, but I don't think either of us can handle whatever it is you're going to tell me without some wine."

She got up, disappeared into the kitchen, returned less than a minute later with two glasses filled to the brim in one hand, and two bottles, one of them unopened, in the other.

It took both of those bottles, and then a third, for him to get through the long list of Robert's sins against him, his parents, his old girlfriends, and the world at large. When he was done, Sheryl asked, "Do you have any idea what he wants now?"

He shook his head. "Not a clue. I presume he's jealous of me, since I'm sure our mother told him all about my job here and how well everything is going for me."

"Yeah, I got that impression from him." Sheryl proceeded to describe her conversation with Robert, which was exactly what he expected: plenty of complaining about him, plenty of insults, and nothing about Robert himself, because, really, what did Robert have to say about himself that any decent person would want to hear?

"Interesting," he said when she was done. "Perhaps he's slipping a bit. I'd have thought he would have been more subtle. He turned Grace against me that way." Grace had been his first girlfriend, sophomore year of high school. The first girl he'd ever properly kissed, too. But Robert put an end to it, and Jon had never even had the chance to plead his case to the girl.

"Well, he didn't know I'm your..." He didn't think Sheryl was fishing for him to say the word; she, like him, honestly didn't know what they were to each other. But it was time to change that. In the movies, wars and crises were opportunities for people to declare their feelings while they could, knowing that tomorrow wasn't guaranteed to them.

"Girlfriend. That's the word you're looking for, Sheryl. You're my girlfriend." She sat there for a moment, then another, absorbing it, and then she kissed him, and for a while all thoughts of his brother were forgotten.

25.

ARIEL - NOW

"Uncle Robert wasn't really that bad, was he? You said everything worked out because of him, so he must have done something good."

The wine was all gone, and the birthday cake. And the fire was starting to die out. It felt like the evening was ending, but Ariel didn't want to go to bed before her parents got to the end of the story.

Her father must have been reading her mind. "We're getting to that. But we are not barbarians. I shall go outside and bring in more firewood. Sheryl, you get the coffee started, and see if you can find that bottle of Amaretto we bought last month. And Ariel, go into the pantry, I believe there's a package of Oreos stuffed in there somewhere." He got up, headed for the front door, stopped with his hand on the doorknob. "Sheryl, please be gentle with the lever on the espresso machine."

Her mother sighed theatrically. "It's been twenty-five years, Doc! Are you ever going to let me forget the time I broke the machine?"

Her father mumbled something that might have been "sorry." He didn't need to apologize; her mother had broken the machine many times. It was uncanny, really. No matter how careful she was - and Ariel had been there watching her on several occasions - something went wrong with the espresso machine nearly every time her mother tried to use it.

This time, though, it worked perfectly. Maybe the appliance gods were showing mercy in honor of her birthday. Her mother returned from the kitchen with three cups, Ariel found the Oreos, and her father had the fire roaring again.

"This is where things get weird," her mother said, when they were all seated together on the sofa. Ariel wondered - she'd never asked - if it was the same $9,000 sofa her mother had had imported from France. "I didn't even write all of it down, because it was too hard to believe, and if I couldn't believe it after it happened to me, who else would?"

There was no point mentioning that, since the diary was for her, it didn't really matter if anyone else believed any of it.

"It's been pretty weird already, Mom."

"Well, you just wait, young lady," her father said. "The best is yet to come…"

26.

SHERYL - THEN

The week was almost over, and there had been a distressing lack progress on all fronts.

Sheryl was no closer to figuring out how to deal with Maribeth's shares at next Monday's Starwood board meeting. Her boyfriend - the one good thing this week was that she could say it now, and mean it - was no closer to figuring out what his brother might be up to. And even though they were officially dating now, they hadn't actually managed to spend anything in the way of quality time together, between her company, his job and plotting against their enemies.

Thursday morning, though, right before lunch, there was a development. Sheryl was walking back from the bathroom, and the light in her office was on, even though it was on a motion sensor and could only have been turned on by someone else and nobody else had permission to go in there except for her.

"I see you got rid of the dust bunnies," Annalise Starwood said, when Sheryl walked into her office. Just like last time, she had her feet up on the desk, and today they were clad in a pair of Jimmy Choos that Sheryl knew cost $4,000 because she'd seen them in the Lord & Taylor catalog last week.

"I'm glad you approve of my housekeeping," she answered. "May I ask why you're here today?" What Sheryl wanted to ask was, why couldn't Annalise just call like a normal person? Why did she have to show up unannounced, like she was Batman or something? But of course to even pose that question was to answer it.

"I have a gift for you." Annalise held up a key - a car key, by the looks of it - and placed it down on her desk. Sheryl had a monthly planner calendar on her desk, and the key had been laid neatly inside the square for this upcoming Saturday.

"That's the key for the Rolls?"

Annalise laughed. "Believe it or not, Father keeps the key in the safe in his office. You see, he will not drive the Rolls in anything but perfect conditions, so in order to avoid the temptation of taking it out on a day that's too cloudy, or too sunny, or when his horoscope isn't promising, or whatever else passes for a reason in his mind, he keeps the key locked away."

Sheryl started to ask how Annalise got into Noah's safe, but she caught herself. "Of course you've got the combination to his safe." Maybe she actually *was* Batman. That was exactly the kind of thing he did in the movies, wasn't it? "But what am I supposed to do with it?"

Annalise gave her a withering state, the same look that Sister Carmelita directed towards her back in second grade. "Using the Rolls was your idea. I expect you'll figure out some way to use it to Maribeth's disadvantage."

The key to the Rolls certainly made things easier. "But I still don't have the key to the garage. Besides, how am I supposed to do anything with your father in the house?"

Annalise was enjoying this. Sheryl imagined that as a child, she pulled the wings off of flies just to watch them suffer. She probably still did. "Father carries the key to the garage on his person, so you'll have to come up with a way of getting into the garage on your own. But you are a resourceful woman, I'm sure you can manage that. And as for your second objection, Father will be going out of town tomorrow, and returning late Sunday night."

She could have just said that up front, rather than making Sheryl feel stupid for asking. But, she supposed, lions never changed their spots. Or stripes, or however that phrase went.

"I'll do my best," she told Annalise. That was the wrong response, because the withering look returned.

"Oh, no. Your best isn't nearly good enough. I expect success. Otherwise, I will have to pay you another visit after the board meeting on Monday, and neither of us wants that."

If worse came to worse, she supposed she could find herself a sledgehammer and smash the garage door open. It would hardly be subtle, but this was not a time for subtlety anyway.

Even with access to the car, though, there was still the question of how Maribeth could be blamed for whatever might happen to it.

There was also the question of what, exactly, *should* happen to it. She was no automotive aficionado, but you didn't have to be to appreciate a Rolls Royce. Damaging it would be like defacing a great work of art. And considering Noah's feelings towards it, even cosmetic damage might give the old man a heart attack. Whatever her feelings towards him, Sheryl did not want that on her conscience.

There had to be some solution. Maybe Jon would be able to come up with something, now that she had a way to get to the Rolls. She could go over to the hospital right now and ask him.

It turned out that she didn't have to. She got as far as the lobby, when she saw Jon, marching in through the front door of the building, a determined glint in his eye.

"You look like a man on a mission," she said, and he didn't answer. He grabbed her hand, turned around and led her outside and then all the way around the building to the loading dock in the back.

"I am. But the walls have ears. I don't trust your office any more than mine."

27.

JON - THEN

He knew he sounded paranoid. Worse, he knew he sounded exactly like Sheryl in her most manic moments. But sometimes paranoia was called for, and the presence of his brother definitely qualified as one of those times.

"What - you think somebody is spying on you?" Sheryl didn't dismiss it entirely out of hand, but she also didn't sound totally convinced.

"Not somebody. My brother. And I don't think he is, I know he is." It was unlike Robert to be so clumsy, but perhaps he was overconfident. Or merely out of practice; it had been three years since his last attempt to ruin Jon's life, after all.

"How do you know? And can we talk somewhere where there's not loud machinery and smelly trucks?"

"No, because it'll be harder for him to overhear if he's spying on you, too."

She held up a hand, and she was clearly making an effort not to roll her eyes at him. "Hold up. Just hold up a minute. Why do you think he's spying on you?"

He wouldn't have believed it himself, had he not seen the proof. Not because Robert was above that sort of thing, but simply because he'd never showed the mechanical aptitude to pull off something like planting a recording device in a telephone.

He explained to Sheryl how he'd discovered the bug. It had been a complete accident. Not two hours ago, Monique had knocked the phone handset onto the floor just as he'd been walking past, on his way back from the bathroom. He'd picked it up for her, and that's when he spotted the little device plugged into the back. Or, more accurately, he saw the phone line plugged into the little device, and then the device into the jack on the back of the phone.

"It looked like it didn't belong there, but it's not as though I installed the phones myself, and I'm no electronics expect. I allowed myself to think that perhaps it was part of the phone, and it had been there all along."

"What did you do?"

Exactly what Sheryl would have done in his place, most likely. "I stopped by Tabitha's office and made a point of looking closely at her receptionist's desk, and, lo and behold, there was no device there."

Sheryl nodded along at that. "But how do you know your brother put it there?"

Jon sighed. He was telling this all out of order. Robert always managed to rattle him. "Right. Let me back up. He came looking for me in my office. Monique told me. She came back from lunch, and she saw him lurking outside my door, so he introduced himself and then he left. But he'd accomplished his mission."

"Did you get rid of the bug?"

He was surprised at the question. He would have expected her to see this for the opportunity it was. "Of course not! If I did that, he'd know I found it. I left it there, and now we can use it against him."

Sheryl perked up at that idea. "We can feed him false information! I love it! But - what exactly do we want him to hear?"

That was the part he hadn't figured out. Spreading disinformation was only useful if you knew what the disinformee actually wanted in the first place, so you could throw them off the track. But he had no clue what Robert was planning.

"There's the rub."

Sheryl started to answer him, but she was drowned out by the garbage truck backed up to the building. A dumpster was being unloaded into it, and aside from the godawful noise, the stench was unbelievable. This was ridiculous. There had to be someplace better to talk without fear of being overheard. He grabbed her hand and led Sheryl away from the trash.

"Thank you! Now I remember why I never come back here!" It took her a moment to realize she didn't need to shout over the noise. "Let's go up to my apartment. I'm sure your brother doesn't have it bugged, too."

"Annalise broke into your apartment."

"Annalise is in league with the devil. I don't think your brother ranks as high. I'm sure we'll be fine there." That was probably true on all counts. But he did insist that they walk a circuitous route, rather than the quicker way, straight down Fourth St. until they hit Galley St. then over to Second.

It took forty minutes, but Jon didn't mind. The walk gave him time to clear his head and try to think more rationally about everything. His silence made Sheryl suspicious, though. She tapped his forehead. "What's going on in that brain of yours, Doc?"

"Nothing, unfortunately," he said. At least she was still holding his hand. That definitely helped. "I keep hitting a brick wall. I know he's here to cause me grief, but I can't guess how." Sheryl opened her mouth, but he held his free hand up. "I know what you're going to say, and I thought about it myself. That maybe he isn't here for nefarious purposes. But here's the thing. He knows where I work. If he were here for a good reason, wouldn't he have left a message, or waited for me to come back from lunch?"

No, he came to the office specifically to plant the listening device. Which brought him right back to the question of why. Did he want to get Jon fired, and he hoped that he might overhear something that would serve as ammunition? Did he hope to overhear Jon talking to Sheryl, then use whatever he learned to steal her away somehow?

"You've got a point," she said, as they entered her building. Thankfully, when they got up to her apartment, there was nobody lurking inside; it was blissfully empty.

Blissful. Now there was a dangerous word to be thinking about, standing in her living room, holding her hand. Not that it was an unwelcome one; to the contrary, he could feel just how welcome it was. But this wasn't the time, and things between them were still too fragile. Once they sorted out his brother, and her problems with Maribeth, *then* they could explore the idea of blissfulness in loving detail.

Speaking of the Maribeth problem, Sheryl was doing exactly that, interrupting his thoughts. "Since we've hit a dead end with your brother, maybe we should talk about how I'm going to use the key to the Rolls Royce to turn Noah Starwood against Maribeth." He just looked at her blankly. All of that was news to him. "It's like you told me that time, Doc. If you get stuck on a problem, sometimes the best thing to do is put it aside and focus on a different problem, and let your unconscious mind work on the stuck thing in the background. Right?"

Yes, he had said that to her, hadn't he? "Right. But could you back up and tell me exactly what in God's name you mean about the key to Noah Starwood's Rolls Royce?" She did, and the story was every bit as horrible as he'd imagined it would be.

"No, Sheryl. I will have nothing to do with that. First, damaging a Rolls Royce Silver Phantom would be like slicing up the Mona Lisa with a razor blade. Second, stealing a car worth half a million dollars is a major felony. And, third, you wouldn't have to worry about getting arrested because Noah would kill you himself." It was probably worth more than half a million, for all Jon knew. The actual amount didn't matter, though, because its value to Noah was beyond any possible monetary figure.

"Spoilsport!" She said it mostly playfully, or at least he hoped so. "That was the only good idea I had! If we don't do something with the car, what else is there to make sure the vote goes Annalise's way on Monday?" Apparently, it *wasn't* mostly playful.

"I don't know, Sheryl. I would suggest you try to reason with Annalise, but even I know that would be a fool's errand."

Sheryl didn't reply; instead, she disappeared into the kitchen and returned five minutes later with two cups of coffee. "I figured this would be better than wine, since we've got some heavy thinking to do. I know it's not $1,400 coffee, but it's not too bad, is it?"

It wasn't, truth be told. "It's quite good, Sheryl."

She didn't appear to hear him. She sat there, her cup halfway to her lips, and that faraway look in her eyes she got when she was straining to recall something. "Koffee! The Koffee Hut!" He just stared at her. "You said that your brother always tries to ruin your relationships, right?" She didn't wait for an answer. "He talked to me for half an hour, and he had no idea we're dating. Or whatever we're doing. And I didn't let on, and Krista didn't either, she kept her big mouth shut for once in her life, thank God."

That was good news, but he didn't see how it really helped. "And?"

"And, don't you see?" She was looking at him the way you looked at someone who couldn't quite manage to put two and two together to get four.

"Sadly, I do not."

"Oh, my God, Doc! And you're the psychiatrist?" He didn't respond to the insult to his professional competence, but she was on a roll now and probably wouldn't even have heard him anyway. "He doesn't know we're together. And he always wants to mess things up for you. Isn't it obvious?" He drank his whole cup of coffee in two swallows, but it provided no answers, obvious or otherwise. "We convince him that you're dating Maribeth! And then we set it up so that they're in the same place, and we make sure Will is there to see them together! It's perfect!"

It was far from perfect. In his opinion, it was a bad idea on every level. But he could think of no idea that was better; or, sadly, any kind of idea at all.

28.

ARIEL - NOW

"Mom, you didn't write about the Rolls Royce in the diary. What did you do to it?" Ariel knew it couldn't have been anything permanent. "I mean, I know you didn't wreck it, because Elizabeth's father gave it to her for *her* twenty-first, and she invited me along to take it for a drive last week."

Elizabeth Starwood had been given the insanely expensive car by her father, Brad, who in turn had inherited it from Noah when he'd passed away a few years ago.

"Seriously? Brad gave it to her as a gift?" Her mother was dumbfounded, which didn't happen very often. "He really wanted to ruin her for every boy she'll ever meet, didn't he?"

Ariel didn't understand, but her father got it immediately. "It's brilliant. I have to give the man credit." He turned to

Ariel. "How can any potential boyfriend possibly measure up compared to that? How could any gift top a Rolls Royce for her birthday?"

There was, she supposed, some logic to that. But it didn't answer her real question. "Forget about Mr. Starwood's motives. What did you do to the car back then?"

"Nothing, really." But her mother couldn't look her in the eyes as she said it.

Ariel just sighed, deeply, as did her father. "The whole truth, Sheryl."

Her mother threw up her hands in surrender. "Fine, I'll tell you. But I just have to say first, technically, I didn't personally do anything to it. It was your Uncle Robert. I merely created a situation in which things happened that I had no direct involvement in." That was an impressive use of the passive voice, even for her mother.

"So you did do something! I knew it!"

Her mother sighed. "Who's telling this story, you or me?" She didn't wait for Ariel to respond. She rarely did. "Right, me. So let me tell it. Like your father said, we figured out that we could trick your Uncle into thinking that he was dating Maribeth, and it was a brilliant idea, if I do say so myself."

"You figured it out, Sheryl." She could understand why her father wanted no part of the responsibility for it, even almost twenty-five years later. "As I recall, I was opposed to the idea."

"Anyway," her mother went on, entirely ignoring her father's protest, "we figured it out, and then…"

29.

SHERYL – THEN

She knew Jon would not approve of what she was about to do, but she could see no better alternative. If it worked out, it would benefit him just as much as her, and when all was said and done, he would thank her. Of course, he'd probably yell at her first. Or glare and glower; he wasn't really a yeller.

If it didn't work, well, she could burn that bridge when she got to it. In the meantime, she had a fake phone message to deliver.

Sheryl had jotted down notes, something she never did. But she'd also never made a fake call to a bugged phone before, and it seemed wise to be prepared.

She was sitting on her sofa. Sheryl had started out in her bedroom, but impersonating Maribeth while lying on her own bed felt weird, so the living room it was. She picked up the phone, dialed Jon's office, and waited through the recording of his receptionist greeting after-hours callers. Then came the beep, and showtime.

"Jon, this is Maribeth." She had practiced for nearly an hour, and she was proud that she'd gotten her archenemy's voice down. The first few tries had been awful, but after twenty or thirty times through, she thought it might even fool Maribeth's fiancé. It was definitely good enough to fool Jon's brother, who, presumably, had never actually spoken to the woman.

"I need you to do me a favor. I left my car over at the Starwood mansion, in the garage around the back. It'll be open, and the key's in the ignition. Can you go pick it up and drive it to my office tomorrow afternoon?"

Yes, she and Jon had agreed on the idea of making his brother think that he was dating Maribeth, and then somehow maneuvering him into close quarters with her and making sure Will Starwood saw them together. But after Jon had gone home, she'd reconsidered things. Wouldn't it all work better if the Rolls Royce was used in the plan, too?

Of course it would. It was perfect. Jon's brother would hear the message via his listening device, and, ideally, having no reason not to believe it was genuine, he'd act on it. He would try to steal his brother's thunder by going to the Starwood mansion, taking the Rolls, and driving it over to Starwood Industries headquarters, so impressing the woman whom he believed was Jon's girlfriend that she would throw Jon over for him.

In reality, what would happen, assuming all went well, would be an epic meltdown in the lobby of Starwood Industries headquarters with Noah and Maribeth both in the lobby when Robert drove up in Noah's "borrowed" car.

Phase three of the plan was ensuring that both Noah and Maribeth would actually be there in the lobby at the appointed time.

Sheryl knew that Noah would be in the office tomorrow afternoon. Vanessa had a friend who worked as a secretary just down the hall from Noah's office, and she'd confirmed both that the old man was leaving town, just as Annalise had said, but also that he'd be spending most of the day in the office before he departed.

From her office window, Sheryl looked down on Fourth St., and she'd be able to see the Rolls driving straight up and past her building on its way to Starwood. The moment she saw it, she'd pass the word to Vanessa, who'd pass the word to her friend, who would concoct some sort of "emergency" that required Noah's immediate attention in the lobby. At the same time, Sheryl herself would call Maribeth, under the pretense of an apology for all the upset Sheryl had caused her over the past few months.

And then, with all the pieces in place, the conclusion was inevitable: Robert would park the car right in front of the big revolving door that led into the Starwood lobby, and he'd walk through it and call out for Maribeth. Maribeth would be shocked, and Noah would lose his mind, throw Maribeth out of the building, probably call the police on Robert, and all would be right with the world.

Except, when she thought about it like that, all laid out step-by-step, Sheryl had to admit that the plan was not quite as airtight as it had seemed when she was dreaming it all up. Honestly, it felt more like one of the plans the Coyote always came up with in the old Road Runner cartoons. But what other choice did she have?

None. She had no other choice. Maribeth wasn't going to voluntarily give up her job at Starwood. Will wasn't going to suddenly realize his fiancée was a loathsome, deceitful cow. Noah wasn't going to change his vote in the board meeting for no reason. And Annalise wasn't going to forget her promise to destroy Mirage, and Sheryl if she didn't get her way.

So it was this - Acme dynamite and all - or nothing.

The clock read one o'clock in the morning, and it was time to put phase two of the plan into action. This was the most dangerous part of the whole thing, but there was no way around it.

Sheryl got dressed - all in black, which was *so* not her color, but desperate times and all that - locked up her apartment, took the elevator down to the parking garage and walked over to her Miata. With every step, her footsteps echoed back at her, and so did all her doubts. But she was committed to the plan, she had to see it through.

The roads were deserted at this hour, leaving her alone with her thoughts. It didn't help that the one station she could tune in on the radio was playing "Love in the Balance," a call-in show where listeners sought advice on their romantic dilemmas. It especially didn't help that the first caller was a man who wanted to know whether he should dump his girlfriend because she compulsively kept secrets from him. It was almost as though the universe was trying to send her a message.

If it was, she didn't pay it any heed.

She parked about a quarter of a mile from the turn into the Starwood driveway, and made her way up to the house on foot. It seemed best to leave the car out of sight. Anyway, there shouldn't be anyone walking around to see her as she made her way to the house. And there weren't any dangerous animals out here. At least, she didn't think there were. What kind of carnivorous animals could there really be, anyway? There were no bears or wolves in the Hudson Valley, right? They lived somewhere else, out west, or maybe in Maine, or wherever. Didn't they? The nature shows she liked to watch were always set in faraway, exotic locations. Surely she was safe here from being clawed or bitten or whatever else dangerous animals did.

Anyway, the real danger was people, and she'd done what she could to make it harder for any of them to spot her. She crouched down as she walked towards the house, and as she got closer, she saw that there were no lights on anywhere on the first floor. There was one on the second, but she knew which window that was – the hallway bathroom. That light was always kept on, according to the story she'd been told, because Tabitha insisted on it. And the reason she insisted was that one morning she'd gone in there and there'd been urine all over the floor, and Will had blamed it on not being able to see where he was aiming in the dark. Which just went to prove that rich people really were just like everyone else, at least in the most disgusting ways.

There was one other light on, a room on the third floor that she knew belonged to Joseph, who had always liked to read well into the early morning hours. So it was nothing to worry about.

She continued creeping up to the house, and then around the back, still unobserved, until she reached the garage that housed the prized Rolls Royce.

It wasn't too late. She could still turn back. She could retreat to her car, drive home, call over to Jon and apologize - she'd have to wake him up, which would mean two apologies, but she could still do it. It was what any sensible person would do. It was what the woman that she wanted to become - for Jon - would do.

No.

This was who she was. Not the woman who retreated like a coward just because some people might call her plan reckless, or irresponsible, or entirely insane. Absolutely not. She was the woman who would go to any lengths to defend herself, and her company, and, heck, her boyfriend, too.

She wanted Jon to see that she'd go to extremes for him, not just for herself. And the truth was, if his brother wasn't involved, if she didn't have something to prove to him, she might turn around and go home and hope against hope that Annalise might show her some mercy.

But his brother was involved, and she wasn't turning around and going home.

None of it would matter, though, if she couldn't open the lock on the garage. But she'd planned for that, too. She'd stopped by the public library yesterday, shortly before they closed for the day, and checked out a book on how locks worked. It wasn't technically a manual on how to pick locks, but the topic was discussed, and the illustrations were very clear. Besides, the technique she'd gleaned from the book had worked on her bedroom door.

It worked here, too. She heard the tiny click of the lock opening, a sound that was barely audible and yet impossibly loud at the same time. But surely that was just her imagination. It had to be.

She waited a couple of minutes to be sure, then she turned the doorknob and pushed open the door. Slowly, inch by inch, she stepped inside, and as soon as she was past the threshold, she saw a problem. A big one.

There was a panel on the wall, right at eye level. An alarm panel.

At first glance, it looked the same as the alarm panels she remembered from her brief stint living at the mansion. But that had been three years ago. Could it really be the same? And even if it was, could the code still be the same?

She'd been given the code at the time, and she still remembered it. It wasn't a hard number to remember – 1121, Eleanor Starwood's birthday. She pushed the numbers, then the disarm button, then she closed her eyes and held her breath.

Five seconds, ten, fifteen, and Sheryl finally exhaled, but she still didn't dare look at the panel. There was silence, but that didn't necessarily prove anything, because it might be a silent alarm.

Now or never. She opened her eyes and saw a beautiful sight: little green letters. Friendly little green letters, flashing gently.

DISARMED

Maybe the universe wanted her to succeed after all.

30.

JON – THEN

Jon awoke to the sound of banging on his front door, accompanied by the voices of men with British accents demanding he open up at once. It took him a moment to realize the sounds were all in his head. Nobody was actually pounding on his door; it was a memory from a dream.

He rarely remembered his dreams, but this one was hard to forget. A whole squad of guards from Buckingham Place trying to smash down one's front door was about as memorable as it got. He could see them in his mind's eye, with the red coats and the big black hats, banging their swords against his door.

It didn't take a degree in psychiatry to understand what the dream had been about. It was a direct result of his research at the public library yesterday. He'd spent an hour searching until he found what he was looking for: a book about the history of Rolls Royce and the various models they'd produced over the years. And he now knew exactly which model of Silver Phantom Noah Starwood owned. Even more, he knew exactly which car out of that production line the man owned.

That knowledge that made it vital to get to the hospital as early as possible this morning, so he could remove Robert's listening device before Sheryl could do anything rash. She had no idea how much fire she was playing with, or how hot it was.

He skipped breakfast, drove to work rather than walked, and he made it to his office at exactly 7:09 AM. The device was removed at 7:10 and smashed into a thousand tiny plastic and metal bits at 7:11.

He contemplated his handiwork for another couple of minutes before he noticed the little orange light blinking on Monique's phone, indicating there was a message. He picked up the handset gingerly, as though it were a live hand grenade, and pushed the button to play the message with his breath held and his entire body tensed up, the way he imagined it would feel cutting the green wire to defuse a bomb.

The message played, and the moment he heard Sheryl's voice - she did a decent job of imitating Maribeth, but not nearly good enough to fool anyone who actually knew her - his heart sank. As he listened to the whole thing, he felt himself shaking uncontrollably. This was beyond bad. It was so much worse than he'd imagined as the worst-case scenario.

What made it tragic, on top of everything else, was that he knew she believed in her heart, with every fiber of her being, that she was doing not only the right thing, but the only possible thing under the circumstances.

Now he'd have to save her from the consequences of her mad plan. And himself, since it seemed impossible that he would escape blame from Noah Starwood. And, God help him, his brother, too.

On the drive over to the Starwood mansion, Jon argued with himself over what to do about Sheryl, once the danger was past.

Obviously, he should cut his losses and break things off with her once and for all. She was never going to change, never going to behave with even the vaguest sense of responsibility or regard for the consequences of her actions.

Equally obviously, he would never, not in a million years, find someone who was as passionate as her, as willing to commit a hundred percent - hell, a thousand percent - to the things, and the people, that were important to her.

But surely there were other passionate women out there, women who would never think to steal a car worth well over a million dollars in order to settle a personal grudge with a business rival.

That was unquestionably true, but it was also, troubling as it was to admit, insanely sexy. He couldn't help what he felt; the heart wanted what the heart wanted, and nothing could change that. Besides, as a psychiatrist, wasn't he the perfect person not to change her, but to help her redirect her passion to more constructive ends?

He went back and forth, but the argument was already decided, had been decided before it even started. He wasn't going to break it off with her; if he had any intention of doing that, he wouldn't be driving over to the Starwood mansion. He'd have called Noah from his office, thrown Sheryl under the bus and washed his hands of the whole situation. Instead, here he was, pulling to a stop and parking about a quarter-mile from the turn into the Starwood driveway.

When he got out of the car, he smelled something - oil, perhaps?

Yes, oil. There was a small puddle right under his car, but it wasn't from his car. Sheryl's Miata had a small oil leak that the mechanics at the shop hadn't been able to fix. She'd gone on about that for a good half hour a couple of weeks ago, and she'd been quite creative in her curses upon the repairmen who'd disappointed her so.

The oil proved one thing beyond any doubt: he and Sheryl were clearly destined for each other. It was superstitious nonsense, of course, but how else to explain that he parked in precisely the same spot she'd used last night?

He followed her path to the house, which was *not* further proof of destiny; there wasn't any other way to go. It wasn't quite eight o'clock yet, and he hadn't thought through how he'd explain himself if any of the Starwoods or their household staff spotted him, but, luckily, none of them did.

He saw no one at all until he made his way around the back of the house, and was within sight of the garage. And then he did see someone.

His brother.

His brother, lying on the ground, unconscious, with a welt on the back of his head that Jon could see from twenty feet away. This time, there was no extended argument with himself. Regardless of what he felt about Robert, they *were* brothers, and you didn't leave your brother lying there unconscious to take the fall for the theft of an incalculably valuable automobile.

Thank God Robert had kept his weight down. He had many flaws - too many to count, really - but poor fitness was not one of them. Jon was able to lift him over his shoulder for a fireman's carry back to his car. He was out of breath by the time he set his brother down on the ground, propped up against the driver's side door.

Jon knew he should take his brother straight to the hospital, but that would raise too many questions, and he wasn't prepared to brazenly lie to his colleagues. Sheryl would definitely brazenly lie if the situation called for it - but she would also not go to the hospital in the first place, precisely to avoid the same questions Jon was avoiding.

He was starting to think like her. It was terrifying living this way, from one short-sighted decision to the next, trying to stay half a step ahead of problems you created for yourself. How did she manage it?

Never mind. The psychoanalysis could wait. His priority right now was catching his breath, then checking on his brother to make sure he hadn't missed any obvious signs of trauma that would require a trip to the hospital, awkward questions and all.

There didn't appear to be any, although obviously Robert might have a concussion and there was no way to determine that while he was unconscious. But otherwise, he didn't seem to be in any immediate danger.

Robert began to stir. Jon was both curious and terrified to hear what he would say about what had happened to him.

"You?" Robert stared at him with barely-focused eyes. "What - why did you hit me?"

Well, he remembered being hit. That was a good sign. And his eyes were tracking now. Also positive. "Use your brain, you moron." It was probably unfair to say that, considering he still might be concussed. "Sorry. Force of habit. But think it through. If I knocked you out, would I be standing here having such a pleasant conversation with you?"

Robert was usually quick with a comeback, but it took him a moment to process Jon's words. That definitely argued for a concussion. "I - uh - I guess not. Where *is* here, by the way?" Robert looked around, his head turning slowly and gingerly, taking in the trees, the one-lane road, and the general absence of any other people.

Jon gestured vaguely in the direction of the Starwood mansion. "About a quarter mile from where I found you. Do you happen to remember what you were doing there?"

Again, it took Robert a little while to respond. "I was going to get your girlfriend's car, and surprise her." He tried to smile, but it looked more like a queasy grimace. "Show her how a real man treats his woman, you know?" The insult came out half-heartedly.

Sheryl's plan had worked to perfection - other than the slight glitch of whoever knocked Robert out and possibly stole one of the most valuable cars in the world. Robert had completely fallen for her fake message, and he'd done exactly what she'd hoped he would. Even though it had clearly gone wrong, he couldn't help but admire her gift for scheming.

"You knew, didn't you?" Robert's voice was a little stronger now. "You set me up. You and your girlfriend."

If he'd known it was that easy to fool Robert, he probably would have cooperated in the plan. "No, it was all her, I'm afraid. But knocking you out was not planned. You were supposed to get the car." Was the car still in the garage? The only way to find out was to go back there and check, and Jon had no wish to do that now. "You didn't see who hit you?"

Robert opened his mouth for what Jon assumed would be another insult, but he must have thought better of it. Instead, he closed his eyes, presumably straining to summon up a memory to actually answer the question. "No. I thought I heard something behind me, and I started to turn around, and that was it."

It couldn't have been any of the Starwoods, or their employees. If it had been, they would have called the police and had Robert arrested. It was possible Tabitha or Brad might not have, based on his resemblance to Jon, but they'd definitely have brought him into the house to ask some pointed questions. Either way, he wouldn't have been left outside.

"Great. So some random person knocked you out, and then they stole the Rolls Royce Silver Phantom that you were supposed to steal, and God only knows where it is now."

The name of the car seemed to instantly clear all the cobwebs from Robert's brain. "You're joking!"

If only. "I'm afraid not. And it's worse than that. It wasn't just any old Silver Phantom." As though there was such a thing. "It was a Silver Phantom IV."

His brother stared at him with a combination of awe, unabashed greed and terror in his eyes. "No. No way."

That had been Jon's reaction, too, when he'd put it all together and figured out the exact model of Rolls Royce Noah owned.

According to the book he'd found, there had been only eighteen of them made, ever. And of those, only one was unaccounted for - the book reported that it had been sold to someone in Switzerland in the 1960's, and then it was rumored to have been shipped to the United States in 1982. Obviously, that was the car that had been in Noah Starwood's garage until an hour or two ago.

But long before that, it had begun life as a car built to order for royalty. Unless Jon was completely wrong, and when it came to library research, he was never wrong, Noah Starwood was the owner of Silver Phantom number three off the production line, originally built for the Shah of Iran in 1951, and returned to the factory when it proved unequal to the difficult road conditions in his country. "Yes."

"They hand-built each one of them."

"Yes."

Jon had never seen his brother like this before. He was in something close to a religious trance. "They only sold them to heads of state. The first one went to the Queen of England."

"Yes."

He supposed it made sense. Robert had always been a classic car fanatic. Learning he'd been within twenty feet of one of the most legendary cars ever built was a pretty big deal. "And your girlfriend was setting me up to steal it?"

"Yes." He didn't plan to say what came out of his mouth next, didn't have any idea those words were anywhere in his brain. But as soon as he heard them, he knew they were the God's honest truth. "And if we get out of this mess in one piece, I'm going to marry her."

31.

ARIEL – NOW

"Holy crap, Dad! I rode around in a million dollar car?" Ariel had known it was ridiculously expensive, but she'd never imagined it could be worth that much. There was probably no point mentioning that she'd actually driven the million dollar car. Only for ten minutes or so, and only after Elizabeth had asked her three times if she wanted to, but still.

"Probably more like two million dollars these days. Or more, if it ever went up for auction. But, yes. Yes, you did, Ariel," her father said. "I hope you enjoyed it. I never did get the privilege myself."

This was insane. She still couldn't quite believe it was a million – or two million - dollar car, or that it was almost seventy years old, or had once belonged to royalty. She doubted Elizabeth knew, either. Had Brad Starwood even known? She didn't think so. As much as Brad loved his daughter, it was hard to imagine him giving her the Rolls Royce if he knew just how rare and expensive it really was.

But all that was secondary at the moment. She replayed the last part of her father's version of the story in her mind. "Holy crap, Dad! You and Mom stole a two million dollar car?"

Her mother was definitely blushing now, actually blushing, which made this a day to mark down on the calendar. "I resent that! I never stole the car! You heard the story! I just passed on information that led someone else to temporarily borrow it. And, anyway, that would never hold up in a court of law, so I really don't see that it's worth going on about."

"Mom, you promised to tell the truth. Even if you didn't steal it yourself, you tried to set up Uncle Robert for it. Except, if he didn't take the car, who did?" It really was a wonder that her parents hadn't gotten themselves thrown in jail, or killed, or something even worse, before they'd ever had the chance to get married and have her.

Her father sighed. "We're getting to that." He finished his coffee, and stood up. "But I think I need some more fortification if we're really going to talk about who took the Rolls." He didn't sound the least bit enthusiastic about it, and this after teasing her mother all night long about telling the whole truth. Did he have something he was embarrassed about, too?

Her mother noticed. "Get your coffee, and then, yes, let's get to that. There was one thing I always wondered about, and I always thought you were keeping something secret all these years, Jon. The whole truth, right?"

32.

SHERYL - THEN

The alarm went off at seven o'clock, and Sheryl awoke feeling as refreshed as she could ever remember. She'd only gotten five hours or so of sleep, but it had been the most restful, peaceful, well-deserved five hours she'd ever had.

Everything had gone perfectly last night, and the plan was in motion, and by this afternoon, Maribeth Peale would be ruined, Annalise Starwood would be off her back, and Jon would have revenge for all the horrible things his brother had done to him over the years.

She took her time getting ready. She had earned an extra-long shower, and she broke out the fancy, forty dollars a bar soap she'd bought in that little boutique in Paris two years ago. When she was done, she opened up the bottle of champagne she kept in the fridge for a special occasion, and treated herself to a mimosa. Then a second one.

Everything was right with the world. Nothing could possibly bring down her mood. Not until the phone rang, anyway.

It was Monique, Jon's receptionist, and she sounded even snottier than usual. "Ms. Jones? Do you know where Dr. Hardy is?"

The woman didn't even bother with a proper greeting. She'd have to talk to Jon about that.

"I don't," she answered. "But I'm not sure why you're calling around to look for him as though he's late for homeroom."

"It's after eight-thirty," Monique said, impatience dripping from every word. But it couldn't possibly be that late. She hadn't been in the shower that long, had she?

The little digital clock on the microwave read 8:41. Apparently she had. And Jon never, ever missed his appointments. Certainly not without calling into the office to let Monique know so she could reschedule his patients.

"I assume you called his house?" Obviously Monique had, but Sheryl didn't know what else to say.

"And the information desk here as well. But what's strange," and now the snottiness was fading, and something like confusion was creeping into her voice, "is that I think he was here before me, and he left suddenly. The suite door was unlocked, and someone moved my phone on my desk."

Sheryl couldn't guess where Jon might be now, but she knew exactly where he'd gone after he left his office so suddenly, and why. And she had to follow him there, right now, just in case he might still be there.

"I'm sure it's fine, Monique. I'm sure everything is perfectly okay. But I promise I'll call you if I hear from him. Have a nice day." She hung up without waiting for the receptionist to answer; there was no time to lose.

She saw Jon's Volvo parked on the side of the road, right around the spot she'd parked herself last night. She wasn't sure whether to be pleased or angry, relieved or frightened.

She parked the car, and as she got out, she could see that Jon was smiling, and that was all the answer she needed. She didn't need to be angry or frightened. All she needed was to kiss him, right now, as though both their lives depended on it. So she did.

An hour, or more likely just a few seconds later, she heard Jon's brother clearing his thread, and she backed away from her boyfriend. It really did feel good, thinking of him that way.

"What the heck, Jon? Did you turn into a player on me? That's the chick from the coffee shop. Does your girlfriend know you're two-timing her?"

There went the good feelings. Instead, confusion and irritation struggled for control of Sheryl's brain. Irritation won out. "Excuse me. 'Chick?'"

Jon's brother actually had the nerve to laugh at her. "I'm sorry, did I offend you? Broad and dame are out of date. Would you prefer floozy? I think that's still current."

Floozy? She wanted to hit him, but that was probably unhelpful just now. "I'd prefer it if you kept your rude comments to yourself. And what exactly did you mean about Jon's girlfriend?"

He was still laughing. Meanwhile, Jon was still recovering from her kiss, and appeared to have temporarily lost the power of speech. "Wow, you don't know?" He turned to Jon. "I have to say, I'm impressed. You've got two women going and neither one knows about the other? Who are you and what have you done with my brother?"

Jon was mouthing his brother's words, but clearly still was in no state to respond intelligently to them. That was fine; Sheryl was willing and more than able to defend her boyfriend's honor. And the answer to why Robert thought he didn't have that honor anymore was obvious, and she cursed herself for not realizing it days ago.

"You've been here for a couple of weeks. You've been sneaking around, spying on my boyfriend, haven't you?" It was the only explanation. He must have seen Maribeth kiss Jon outside the Firehouse Grille, and assumed she was his girlfriend. "That's pretty creepy, don't you think? Don't you have a job or something to do instead of skulking around like some kind of - I don't know, voyeur?" Was that the right word? She glanced over to Jon, who now seemed to be in more or less full possession of his faculties.

"Exactly, Sheryl. Just like some kind of voyeur, that's my brother." Now he focused on said brother. "And here we were, getting along so nicely, bonding over car talk like a couple of normal guys. And then you had to start acting like yourself again and ruin it."

If Jon and his brother were out here talking, then the Rolls hadn't been taken out of the garage yet.

Maybe, as much as it pained her to think about it, that was for the best. She had been so satisfied when she woke up, she'd felt so triumphant, but she hadn't thought all the consequences through, had she? Yes, Maribeth's name would be mud in the eyes of Noah Starwood if Robert had carried through the plan to its conclusion. But what then? Noah would have Robert arrested. As much as Jon wanted to get back at his brother, surely he didn't want the man in prison. He'd hate himself for it. And, sooner or later – probably sooner - he'd hate her for setting it all in motion.

As it was, Robert knew that he had been fooled, embarrassed in the eyes of his brother, and maybe that was enough revenge for Jon. As for Maribeth, Sheryl could go back, retrieve the key from the garage and plant it in her office, or something. That ought to upset Noah enough to vote against her on Monday, and all would be well.

Except both men were looking at her with the same expression, one she couldn't read. And now Robert was rubbing the back of his head, almost as though it was sore.

Because it was sore. Because all would not be well. Sheryl understood in a flash what must have happened. Well, that wasn't true - what she had just realized made no sense, but it felt true all the same.

"The car is gone, isn't it?"

"We don't know for sure," Jon said, speaking in the sort of calming voice Sheryl imagined he used when a patient was threatening suicide. "But I believe it is gone, yes."

The car *was* gone.

It had taken fifteen minutes to determine that. First, Sheryl had to call over to Starwood Industries and confirm that Noah was in his office. Then Jon had to check with the hospital to verify that both Brad and Tabitha were there.

Assured that no Starwoods remained in the house to spot her - well, except for Annalise, but the whole plan had been her idea in the first place – Sheryl went back, crept around to the garage, and saw for herself that it was empty.

Which of course begged the question, "So who knocked Robert out and stole the car?"

Neither Robert nor Jon had any clue, any more than Sheryl herself did. Although there was one possibility, wasn't there? "It was Annalise." Both Hardy brothers stared at her. "Think about it. She gave me the key. And she told me Noah's schedule. She knew it would be today. Who else could it have been?"

Jon wasn't convinced. "Why, Sheryl? I follow the logic, but why would she double cross you?"

She laughed. "Why did the scorpion cross the road? How should I know why Annalise does anything she does?"

Her boyfriend grinned despite himself and put an arm around her. "The chicken crossed the road. And the scorpion stung the frog. But I take your point."

For his part, Robert was still confused. "Who is Annalise? Do you have three women going at once, Jon? I really did underestimate you."

Again, Sheryl wanted to hit him, but it probably wasn't fair to hit somebody who'd already been knocked out once this morning, no matter how much of a jerk he was. Besides, even if he was a jerk, they needed all the help they could get if they were going to find the Rolls Royce.

Operating under the assumption that there was safety in numbers, all three of them piled into Jon's dark blue Volvo and headed to the only place anyone could think of to try: Kelly's Gas and Go.

Jon and Robert had argued whether Noah would have kept the gas tank of the Rolls full or near empty, since he drove it so rarely. After five minutes of that, Sheryl had shouted at the both of them, "Enough! Do either of you have any other idea where to start looking? No? Then we're going to the gas station and you're both going to stop acting like children." Amazingly, both men had obeyed her. She could only assume that, without even trying, she'd hit on the exact tone of voice their mother must have used when they misbehaved as children. Hey, whatever worked.

When they arrived at Kelly's Gas and Go, there was both good and bad news. The teenager manning the gas pumps *had* seen the Rolls. "Yeah, it was here. Looked like it came right out of a movie. Never saw anything like it in real life before." Annalise was not the driver, however. "I never saw the guy before. He wouldn't get out, he made me pump the gas. And he gave me the creeps. He had this scar over his eye." The teen traced his finger over his own left eye and then all the way back past his ear.

Who could that possibly be? If Annalise had hired someone to steal her father's prized Rolls Royce, a creepy guy with a huge scar seemed like the sort of man she'd pick for the job. And there really wasn't any other explanation, was there? What were the chances that some random creepy guy just happened to be wandering the grounds of the Starwood mansion at the exact time that somebody else was there to steal the car?

"Did you see where he went?"

The teen nodded. "He went left out of here, and he made a right up Fourth St." At which point he would have been out of sight. But the Starwood Industries building was up on Fourth St. It couldn't be a coincidence, could it?

"I believe in coincidences, but this one is a little too unbelievable, don't you think?" Jon must have been reading her mind. Of course he was. And as much as it sometimes drove her crazy, she loved it. And him, and if they got out of this mess in one piece, she'd say it to him, say those three words, in the correct order, for him and God and whoever else might be in earshot to hear.

33.

JON - THEN

"Why not? It's foolproof! Just let me call Noah, and have him come down to the lobby, and he'll see the Rolls, and he'll blame Annalise because who else in his family would take the key, and everything is perfect!"

There were so many jumps in logic in that one remark that Jon couldn't even count them all. "Several reasons, Sheryl. First of all, just seeing his car out in the wild might give him a heart attack, and that would be on our conscience." It ought to be squarely on Sheryl's conscience, but he was here, wasn't he? He'd encouraged her, hadn't he? He was beginning to think like her, was he not? "Second, it's a huge assumption that he'd blame Annalise." Although it really wasn't, was it? Sheryl was right - with the key in the car, a key that normally resided in his safe, and presumably a key that couldn't be easily copied, Noah would have to assume that it was an inside job. And realistically, the odds that he'd blame Tabitha or Brad or Will or the grandsons were not high, and rightfully so. None of them had any motive to betray him by stealing his most prized possession, and none of them - as far as he knew, anyway - knew how to crack a safe. He probably *would* blame Annalise. "Third, do you really want her as your enemy? You said it yourself; she's probably in league with the devil." He knew what Sheryl's answer to that point would be, though, and she delivered it right on cue.

"Maybe, but it solves my problem for now. He'll fire her from the company, or take away her shares, or God knows what else, but she won't be able to ruin Mirage, and she'll be too busy trying to get back in his good graces to come after me for a while. And maybe I can mend fences with her in the meantime." She batted her eyes at him as she said it, which was completely unfair. They were just the perfect shade of light blue, he could look into them all day, and besides, she made a lot of sense.

"Jon! Snap out of it!" Robert's voice did the trick. He turned away from Sheryl's entrancing gaze to look at his brother. "Since when do you let chicks hypnotize you? Mom always says you're the smart brother, but she should see you now."

Sheryl didn't give him the chance to answer that insult. "You call me a chick again and I'll punch your lights out, okay? Just because you're my boyfriend's brother doesn't mean you get to insult me."

She turned her attention back to Jon, giving him a little flip of her hair, which was even worse than the eyes. Everything she did ought to be illegal, or at least require a permit and a thirty-day waiting period. Especially calling him her boyfriend out loud, in front of his brother.

He shook his head, and then again. He had to clear his thoughts; there was serious business afoot. "Let's all leave the insults and the punching until we've figured out what to do."

"Fine," Robert said from the back seat. "I think the floozy is right." He glared at Sheryl. "Sorry," he went on in a tone that could not have been less apologetic, "I meant to say, the girlfriend is right. Call Mr. Big and let him think his daughter stole the car, problem solved."

It was two against one, and, more importantly, Jon could think of no better idea himself. "Fine. Sheryl, I hope your phone is charged."

It was, but it proved to be of no use. She tried Noah's receptionist, his personal office, the office of Vanessa's friend, then the main switchboard, all to no avail. "Well, let's just go there and march on in and start banging on office doors. We're bound to find him sooner or later," she said, after the last fruitless call.

"You're not real big on subtlety, are you?" Annoying as Robert was, he wasn't wrong about that. "How the heck did you end up with my brother?"

Again, she didn't give him the chance to answer his brother. "Well, Robert, if you must know, he's incredibly smart, and perceptive, and patient, and kind, and he has the most gorgeous eyes, and his hair is to die for." Now she turned to him, leaned close, kissed him. And went right on kissing him for what seemed like several minutes. "And he's one hell of a good kisser," she said. "Maybe you should ask him what his secret is, Robert."

For once, his brother was completely, blessedly, speechless.

The Rolls Royce was there, parked in front of the Starwood building. It had attracted a small crowd, which was no surprise. From what everyone said, Noah only took it out once every few months, maybe not even that often.

It was a thing of beauty. He could see why it was the vehicle of choice for royalty and heads of state. The car was metallic blue, and it absolutely gleamed from every possible surface. It was easy to picture the top down, its owner sitting in the passenger seat waving at his subjects while a tuxedoed chauffeur drove him around.

But there was no driver in it now. The creepy, scarred man was nowhere to be seen, nor was Annalise.

There was nothing to do but what Sheryl had suggested, he supposed. March into the building, try to find Noah, and let the chips fall where they may. But it seemed that Robert had plans of his own. He was already out of the car and walking back up Fourth St.

"I'm done," he called back over his shoulder. "I only came here to see how Mom's golden boy was really doing, and you've made a royal mess of your life, but she'll never believe it, so I'm out of here. Good luck with the floozy, bro."

Jon considered, just for a moment, running after him and making him answer for calling Sheryl a floozy. But they had more important concerns at the moment.

The woman who wasn't a floozy was out of the car, too, and halfway to the big revolving door that opened into the Starwood Industries lobby. She, too, called back to him over her shoulder. "Doc, I'm going in. You keep out of sight. Noah doesn't know you, there's no reason for you to get on his bad side." She ran into the building before he could answer.

He only sat there in the car trying to decide whether to follow Sheryl, go after his brother, or stand guard by the Rolls Royce for a second or two, but that was long enough for the question to be answered for him.

There was a sound right outside his window, unmistakable even though he'd never heard it in real life before. It was the sound of a gun being cocked, and it was followed by a gruff voice telling him to "Get out of the car, nice and slow," in a thick Italian accent.

34.

ARIEL - NOW

"Dad? Somebody threatened to kill you?" There hadn't been a word about it in the diary. From her mother's expression, she hadn't known about this part of the story at all.

"The guy that Annalise hired, he was going to shoot you? You never told me that!"

Even twenty-five years after the fact, it was upsetting to imagine some goon holding a gun to her father's head. It looked as though he felt the same; he was as uncomfortable as Ariel had ever seen him.

"Excuse me a moment." He got up again, went to the kitchen again, and this time returned without coffee, but with the amaretto. And then he drank right out of the bottle.

"That's better. So, yes, the guy threatened to shoot me. But Annalise didn't hire him. Nobody did, actually."

That made no sense at all. "So it really was some random thief? But you said that was impossible."

"Yes, Jon," her mother agreed. "It was impossible. And give me that." She took the bottle out of his hands, took a couple of good, long swallows herself. "Much better. Now I'm ready to hear it. Who was he, really?"

Her father took a deep breath, struggled to put a smile on his face, and answered. "Maribeth's brother."

35.

SHERYL - THEN

S he had been joking - well, mostly joking - when she'd said she would bang on every door in the building until she found Noah. But it was turning out to be no joke.

She finally found him in a conference room on the seventh floor, and only after dodging a couple of security guards and a very persistent marketing intern.

"Noah!" Twelve heads, including Noah Starwood's, turned to look at her.

"Someone call security, and have this trespasser removed," Noah said. There was a scramble as half a dozen employees all went for the phone on the little table in the corner.

"Yes," she said, fixing her attention on Noah. "Call security, they're needed downstairs. Someone stole your Rolls Royce, Noah."

For an instant, he locked eyes with her, and she focused on projecting as much sincerity as she could manage back at him. It must have worked, because he shouted, "Meeting adjourned!" and ran for the door. She'd never seen the old man move that fast, not even the night that the smoke alarm had gone off on the second floor near the end of her six weeks as a member of the Starwood family. He didn't even wait for the elevator, he went for the stairs, and she followed him down.

He was running down them, sometimes hopping two or three steps at a time, and she was having trouble keeping up.

When he finally got to the ground floor, he threw open the door, made it a few steps farther, just far enough to be able to see out the front door, and then fell to his knees. He made the sign of the cross, and as she caught up to him, she heard him murmuring a prayer. And this from a man who, from what his family said, hadn't seen the inside of a church since he'd made Confirmation, which had probably been sometime during the Great Depression.

She saw why; the car was still there. But Jon was nowhere to be seen. What could have happened to him?

"Young lady, I would like an explanation."

She had one; she'd been rehearsing it the whole time she'd been searching for him throughout the building. "I was driving to work - I got a late start this morning - and when I turned up Fourth St., I saw your Rolls Royce. I couldn't believe it, I mean, I know how you guard that car with your life, and I was just stunned, and I tried to call you to let you know, and I couldn't get you, and your secretary wasn't picking up, so I thought, you know, I was your daughter-in-law for a little while, I owe it to him to make sure he knows, and I followed it, and here we are."

He wasn't looking at her; his eyes were fixed on the car. "I don't believe you. You've always got some little scheme going. But I suppose I should thank you for letting me know all the same."

He rose from his knees, made his way to the car. The small crowd of Starwood employees who had been staring at it backed away to give him room. But none of them went back into the building.

Noah walked all around it, peering at this and that, touching it gingerly then brushing away the fingerprints with the sleeve of his suit jacket. And then he tried the driver's side door, and it was locked.

"Someone stole my Rolls Royce Silver Phantom, and then got out and locked it and walked away?" That part didn't make any sense to Sheryl either. He raised his voice, calling out to all the employees who had been looking at the car themselves. "Whoever can tell me what really happened and where the person who was driving this car went gets a ten thousand dollar bonus with your next paycheck!"

Normally, Sheryl would have expected such an offer to produce a stampede straight to Noah to tell him something and try to earn the reward. But Noah Starwood was not a normal boss. He saw through lies and BS better than anyone she'd ever met, and he didn't need to add that anyone who made up a story would find a pink slip instead of a bonus in their next pay envelope.

As Noah shouted at his employees, and her, and the world at large, she saw something, a momentary flash arcing through the air off to her left. It might have been light glinting off of something metal, and then it was gone, followed by the tiniest little tinkling sound, barely audible, and apparently heard by nobody but her.

She knew what it had to be, or at least what she hoped with all her heart it was, and when she followed the sound and squinted down at the ground, maybe twenty feet away, there it was, something small and silver. "Noah! Look over there! Is that...?"

He might be seventy years old, but when it came to anything involving his prized car, Noah Starwood had twenty-twenty vision and the reflexes of an Olympic athlete. He spotted the key instantly and sprinted over to it, shoving two of his employees and a passer-by aside on the way. He reached down, grabbed it, looked at it critically for a moment or two, then held it up triumphantly. And then, again, he said a prayer, and sighed the deepest, most relieved sigh Sheryl had ever heard.

For her part, Sheryl could only assume that Jon had gotten the key from the actual thief – but how? He was in good shape, with decent muscles – no six-pack, but also nothing to be embarrassed about – but he was no fighter. She didn't fancy his chances duking it out with a professional criminal, which the thief had to be. Who else would Annalise have hired to steal the car and double-cross her?

She did understand why he would keep out of sight and toss the key where Noah could see it, rather than bringing it to him. As she'd told him, better to stay out of sight and not get himself on Noah's naughty list.

The thing to do now was to go find him. There was no need to tell Noah her theory as to what had happened. He knew perfectly well where he kept the key, and who had access to the safe that had held it. He'd come to the only reasonable conclusion all on his own.

36.

JON – THEN

He felt the gun poking into his back as the man – who did indeed have a scar starting over his left eye and running all the way past his ear, and who was most definitely creepy – marched him around to the rear of the Starwood building. He saw the trash compactor there, past the loading dock, coming closer with his every step, and he couldn't help wondering if that was his final destination.

The man hadn't spoken again since ordering Jon out of the car, but now that they were off the street and out of sight of anyone else, he stopped and ordered Jon to turn around. "I don't like shooting somebody when I can't look 'em in the eye. It ain't classy."

Jon didn't bother to point out that shooting someone you didn't know, for no good reason, wasn't classy either. "I think

I deserve to know why you want to shoot me," he said instead, and he was surprised to hear how calm and even his voice was.

The man shrugged. "What the hell. Truth is, I got nothin' against you. I don't even know you. But my sister, she says she needs my help, she says this chick is causing her grief and can I do something, so I come up here 'cause family is family, you know?" Jon nodded. It seemed the only sensible thing to do at this point. In the movies, people in his situation leapt at their captor, disarming them with a flying kick or somesuch. But he didn't know how to perform a flying kick, and he doubted his reflexes were any match for this – what was he? A thug? A goon? A gangster? Probably all of the above.

"Your sister?" It wasn't Annalise, unless the Starwood family was even more bizarre than he already knew them to be. It couldn't be Tabitha. That left Maribeth, but how could someone who'd gone to a Swiss boarding school have someone like this for a brother? It was amazing that he could even debate the question with a gun aimed at him. Maybe he hadn't truly accepted his situation yet? The human mind reacted strangely under stress; he saw it every day with his patients, after all.

"Yeah. This chick and her makeup company, she's giving Marie all kinds of *agita*. But the thing is, I don't like hurtin' chicks. Or even throwin' a scare into 'em. But you're the boy-friend, and if I shoot you, she'll get the message loud and clear. So I gotta do it." Marie? That was close enough to Maribeth. It had to be her.

"Maribeth is your sister?" All Jon wanted to do was keep the man talking. As long as he was talking, he wasn't shooting, and somebody else might walk back here. Or something else might happen, Jon couldn't guess what, but anything was possible. Miracles did happen, didn't they?

The gunman gave him a look that, to Jon's disbelief, was sad, almost pleading. "Maribeth, can you believe she calls herself that? And with an 'i,' not even a 'y' like a regular person. Like she's ashamed of her family." The man drew himself up, squared his shoulders. "I got nothin' to be ashamed of, nobody in the whole Pagliacchi family does. I never liked how she wanted to run away from us, change her name, pretend she ain't even Italian. Who does that?" Jon could understand perfectly why Maribeth had done it. "But she's still my little sister, I gotta protect her. So, you know, I'm sorry, man, but I gotta…"

The man would never do what he had to do. Before he could finish his sentence, before he could shoot Jon dead, there was a blur behind him, someone running at him. It wasn't until after that someone had leapt at the gunman, and brought him down to the ground, the gunman's head hitting the pavement with a resounding thud, that Jon saw clearly who it was.

"Robert?"

His brother had saved his life. His no-good, nothing-but-trouble, disaster-at-every-turn brother had actually, for real, saved his life. Did that mean he now owed Robert a debt that could never be repaid?

"Don't get all mushy, Jon. You could have left me for the police to find, I couldn't leave town owing you for that. And I don't care how crappy of a brother you are, I couldn't let you get shot by some *Goodfellas* reject."

All the terror that his brain had held in check during the encounter with the man who'd wanted to kill him was suddenly released, and Jon ran to his brother, pulled him up and hugged him tighter than he ever had in his life, all without anything in the way of conscious thought. He heard himself speaking, but he didn't have the presence of mind to know what he was saying, nor was he capable of caring. Robert let himself be hugged for a little while, and Jon's mind began to reassert control just as his brother finally pushed him away.

"Enough already! Let's not get mushy here. We're even, and that's good enough for me." Robert must have seen something, because pointed behind Jon, shook his head and laughed. "Anyway, I'm done here. You enjoy your life with the girlfriend and the floozy and the crazy rich chick. And here comes the girlfriend now. Good luck, bro." It was amazing; he still didn't get it. But that was Robert in a nutshell, wasn't it?

He turned to see what Robert was referring to. Sure enough, it was Maribeth. He turned back to tell Robert, again, how mixed-up he was, but his brother was already gone, and this time probably for good. For her part, Maribeth ran past him without a word, and straight over to the gunman. She bent over his unconscious body and gently stroked his forehead. "Oh, Charlie. What did you do?"

So it was true. The man who'd been about to kill him really *was* Maribeth's brother. Jon bent down next to her, felt for a pulse then listened to his breathing. "He's – well, I can't say for sure how he'll feel when he wakes up, but he's breathing just fine."

She finally looked at him. "I know he must have threatened you, but please don't call the police. He only did it because I asked him for help. I didn't know what else to do, I had to do something about your girlfriend."

"You two have to stop this feud. Sheryl tried to steal Noah's Rolls Royce, you brought a mobster – he is a mobster, right?" Maribeth nodded. "You brought a mobster to town to threaten her, except he decided to kill me instead because he 'don't like hurtin' chicks.'" Sheryl! He hadn't thought about her during the whole encounter. He hadn't dared; he'd put her entirely out of his mind the moment he saw the gun. It was, he supposed, a survival mechanism. If he had thought of her, he probably would have broken down and cried, begged on his knees not to be killed until he could say goodbye to her. God only knew what Maribeth's brother would have done at that point.

But that was done now. There was no more danger, and no need to say goodbye to Sheryl. There was all the time in the world to find her, talk to her, kiss her.

Or even ask her to marry him.

"Jon, I'm sorry. I really had no idea he'd do that. I just wanted him to make her back off."

He heard something like sincerity in her voice. And Sheryl was hardly blameless in this whole mess. Nor was he. Someone had to make the first gesture of peace, right? "I believe you. And I won't call the police. But you have to stop the feud." She took a deep breath, and nodded. She couldn't quite look him in the eye while she did it, but that was fine. Baby steps. "And you need to go into his pockets and see if the key to Noah's Rolls Royce is there."

37.

ARIEL — NOW

There was too much to wrap her mind around. Ariel didn't even know where to begin, what questions to ask. It was all so crazy.

Her mother, on the other hand, knew exactly what question to ask. "It was Maribeth's brother? He knocked out your brother, he stole the car, he was going to shoot you, and it was Maribeth's brother, and you let him go?"

"Yes, Sheryl." He held up his hands defensively, before she could really begin shouting at him. 'But there's more to it. Why do you think she eased up on you after all that happened?"

"Eased up?" Her mother was standing now, her eyes were flashing with anger, but she took a deep breath and sat back down again before she continued. "I guess she did. She was still a royal pain, but it was never that bad afterwards, was it? But why didn't you tell me? How could you keep a secret like that?"

That wasn't like her father; he preached the value of open communication and no secrets all the time. "That *is* kind of a big deal, Dad. I mean, the way you told it, she was faking everything about her life. Maribeth wasn't even her real name."

He gave Ariel a sad smile. "I didn't have the heart to tell your mother." He went over to her mother, took her hands in his. "I love you, Sheryl, but we both know you wouldn't have kept it to yourself if I told you. And she had enough trouble already. Just having a brother like that, I wouldn't wish him on anybody. At least Robert never tried to kill anybody." He thought about that for a moment. "Well, as far as I know, anyway."

"What trouble, Dad? Did old Noah blame her for stealing the car?"

Her mother answered for him. "No. I was right that he'd blame Annalise. He disowned her for a little while, but it didn't last. I think he disowned every one of his children at one time or another."

That explained why Annalise didn't come after her mother once the dust had settled; she had bigger problems to contend with. "So what about Maribeth?"

Before either of her parents could answer, the doorbell rang. Who on Earth would be visiting at one o'clock in the morning?

38.

Sheryl – Then

The part where Noah Starwood was grateful that his prized car was safe appeared to be over. The part where blame and retribution were meted out was about to begin.

"You know something about this, Sheryl. You tell me right now!"

She'd never lied to him back when she was his daughter-in-law. Well, not really. Not about anything important. She doubted she could do it successfully now. But maybe the strict truth would work, even if it was meant to deceive? "I have no idea who stole your car, Noah. I'm just glad it's in one piece."

She held his gaze as she said it, uncomfortable as it was. She could feel his eyes boring straight through hers and into her brain, but after a moment or two, he appeared to be satisfied that what she'd said was true.

"I'm going to find out, and whoever did it is going to regret the day they were born before I'm through with them."

She considered mentioning the key, and asking him if he still kept in his safe, and wondering idly who might have had access to said safe, but it seemed the better part of valor to let him come around to that on his own. "I'm sure you will, Noah. But if you don't mind, I think I've had enough excitement for one day. I'm going to go home now."

She didn't wait for his answer, she turned around and started walking away. It occurred to her that she'd need to get back to the Starwood mansion and pick up her Miata before Noah got back there with the Rolls. There was no chance she could explain away its presence only a few hundred feet from his driveway.

She'd gotten half a block away from the Starwood building when she saw Jon, running towards her, a wild look in his eyes. He said nothing; he just came straight to her, wrapped his arms around her, and kissed her. She felt the energy radiating off of him, the passion, and also something that might have been stress, or fear, or maybe flat-out terror.

He broke the kiss after a few seconds, took her face in his hands and just stared at her, with an expression that made her think of a starving man who just got brought into the banquet hall. She wanted to know what had happened to him, what was behind that kiss, which she was still shaking from, but she had enough presence of mind to focus on the business at hand first. "There's plenty of time for more of that, but we need to go get my car, right now, before Noah gets home. If he sees it there, well, I don't know what he'll do, but I don't want to find out."

———

"So what happened to you after we split up back there?" The Miata was back in its parking spot in the parking garage of Sheryl's building. Noah had not seen it, they'd gotten away cleanly, and all was right with the world. It was especially right sitting here on her $9,000 French sofa, with Jon next to her, his arm around her.

"I caught up to the guy Annalise hired. Well, I say that, but he didn't get the chance to say anything one way or the other."

Well, that was downright heroic. Her boyfriend fighting to protect her from Annalise's scheme and Noah's wrath? No woman on Earth was as lucky as her. "You beat him up and got the key back? I'm impressed, Doc!" She was more than impressed. If she was being honest, she was pretty aroused, too, and why shouldn't she be honest with Jon about that? There was nothing in the world stopping them from acting on it.

"Not exactly." What did that mean? Did he somehow talk the thief into giving up the key? That was, if anything, even sexier than simply beating the guy up. "It was my brother. I caught up to the guy, but before I could say a word, Robert came flying out of nowhere, tackled him and knocked him right out."

OK that was a little disappointing. But on the other hand, he admitted it to her when no other man she'd ever known would have confessed to it. Because he loved her, and because he knew that she loved him, so he could tell her absolutely anything. And that was the sexiest thing of all.

He had to feel the same way, but if he did, why was he now pushing her away? Why was he backing away from her? Why was he getting down on his knees?"

She knew why. There was only one reason any man would do that. "Yes! Yes, absolutely, definitely, positively yes!"

He laughed at that, and she could see him struggling mightily not to roll his eyes at her. "Sheryl, would you please let me ask the question first?"

39.

JON – THEN

She'd said yes again, and then there'd been a long overdue celebration. And another. And then still another. And then they got dressed again, and Jon cobbled together the best dinner he could manage from the meager contents of Sheryl's pantry while she lit every candle she could find and opened a bottle of champagne.

When they sat down to eat, he asked her, "So how does it feel to be the future Mrs. Hardy?"

She gestured towards the bedroom. "You have to ask, after what we did in there?"

No. Not at all. "Just making sure. You know I like to be thorough." They'd both been quite thorough. Except in one regard. He hadn't told her about Maribeth, or her brother, or that he'd agreed not to call the police.

He had promised Maribeth. And Sheryl wouldn't understand. Maybe someday; she was a lot more willing to stop and think things over now than she'd been when they first met, but he didn't think she was willing to bury the hatchet with her nemesis just yet. Hearing that Maribeth's brother had threatened to shoot him would only make Sheryl want revenge, and start the whole cycle over again.

Much better to keep Maribeth's secret, and keep the peace. Anyway, there were much more important things to think about just now. There was the filet mignon Bearnaise to enjoy.

Well, not exactly filet mignon; Sheryl had a box of steak sandwich patties in her freezer. And not a proper Bearnaise, but it really wasn't that far off even if she'd only had dried onion flakes rather than the shallots the recipe called for.

She seemed to be enjoying it regardless, although that might have been leftover positive feelings from the bedroom. Anyway, now that they were engaged, they could discuss her moving into the Chalet, where there was a real chef's kitchen and a pantry that was always well-stocked and a spice rack that had everything a serious cook could ever ask for.

"You know, Doc, we might have to talk about living arrangements. I love my condo, and I've got the best view, but your kitchen blows mine out of the water." She often remarked that he seemed to read her mind, and here she was doing it to him. It was disconcerting, but also, he had to admit, awfully attractive.

40.

MARIBETH – NOW

Maribeth wondered if she shouldn't have just gone to a hotel. But the lights were on and she could hear muffled voices inside.

After a moment, she heard footsteps approaching, and then the door opened. There was Jon Hardy, and he'd barely changed at all. He might have a little bit less hair and a little more of a waistline, but overall the years had been kind to him.

He ushered her in, and, like him, the Chalet didn't seem to have changed much at all. Nor had his wife - at least, Maribeth assumed they were still married, if they were home together after midnight. She'd aged even more gracefully than he had. Surgery had to have been involved at some point, but whoever had done it had done a fantastic job.

And there, on that same old sofa, was a beautiful dark-haired, bright-eyed girl who had to be Ariel. "Happy birthday!" It was after midnight; technically it was her actual birthday now.

Sheryl Jones, or Hardy, or maybe she had hyphenated, was staring hard at her, but there was less surprise in her eyes than Maribeth would have expected. And neither Jon nor Ariel appeared to be surprised in the slightest.

"We were just talking about you a few minutes ago, believe it or not," Jon said, leading her to the loveseat across from the sofa. "I'd offer you a drink, but we've gone through all the wine, and the amaretto as well. We do have water, if you'd like."

"No thanks. I just came to drop off Ariel's birthday present in person." She ruffled though her purse, pulled out the envelope. "Here. You can go down to Manhattan and use it for a pretty serious shopping spree." Her old self would never have believed the next words out of her mouth, but fifteen years did a lot to change a person. "Maybe you could even use a little of it to buy your mother lunch."

The girl got up, walked over to her, hugged her. She hadn't expected that, but it was – well, it was nice. Her own daughter was fourteen now, and well out of the hugging-her-mother stage. "Thank you! I never knew until tonight, you sent me a check every year for my birthday. So thank you for all those years, too."

"Yes, Maribeth," Sheryl said, and it sounded for all the world like she really meant it. "You didn't have to do that. It was really kind of you. And – well, I guess maybe if things

had been different, maybe things would have been different."
She hadn't changed a bit. "And the truth is, I guess I kind of
wish they had been."

"I think I followed that, Sheryl. And I guess I think I feel
the same." A glass of wine probably would have helped. "But
back up – what did you mean, Jon? Why were you talking
about me?"

Ariel sat herself down next to Maribeth on the loveseat.
"They were telling me the story of how they fell in love. Mom
kept a diary, and she gave it to me, and Dad was filling in
some of the gaps. And they just got finished a little while ago
telling me about…"

Jon interrupted her. "I kept your secret all these years,
Maribeth. Earlier tonight – well, this morning, I suppose -
that was the first time I've ever spoken about it. But now they
both know. About your brother, about everything."

"I believe you," she told him. And she did. He had always
been a man of his word. If he broke it now, well, he'd kept
his promise and her secrets for nearly a quarter of a century.
That was good enough for anybody. "And I really am grateful. But it's fine that they know. It was a long time ago, who
can it hurt now?"

"If you don't mind me asking, what happened to your
brother?" Ariel asked in a nervous voice.

"Nothing good. He's been in and out of prison his whole
adult life. His teenage life, too, come to think of it. I wish it
was different, but he is what he is. I still love him, though.
Family is family." The truth is that he'd been much more in
prison than out; he was in right now, but there was no point

going into all the ugly details. "Back to your parents, you said they were telling you how they got together?"

"Dad just told me how he asked Mom to marry him."

She'd hoped to be married then, too, but her engagement to Will Starwood had fallen through only a few months after the whole mess with her brother and the Rolls Royce. Sheryl and Jon had somehow managed to stay together, though. "I remember. So they didn't tell you about their wedding yet? Or the night you were born? Or how you were kidnapped when you were two years old, and I helped rescue you?"

"Wait, what?" Ariel's jaw dropped, and she stared first at Maribeth, then at each of her parents in turn. "Kidnapped?"

"We were getting to that," Sheryl said. "Probably not tonight. We'll need another couple of bottles of wine for that one."

Jon shook his head. "More than that. We might need a whole case for that story. But, yes, you were kidnapped, and, yes, Maribeth did help save you. And I promise, we'll tell you all about that. Maybe Maribeth will agree to spend the night in the guest room, and one of us can go to the liquor store tomorrow and then she can help us tell the tale?"

"You have to, Maribeth! Please? I know you already gave me a present, but will you stay? A girl only has her twenty-first birthday once."

That was certainly true. "For you, Ariel? Definitely. And I'll just say it now, no matter how unbelievable it's going to sound, it all really happened. I swear."

The end

Sheryl and Jon (and Ariel, and Maribeth, and...)

WILL RETURN IN

"The Lost Princess of Emerald Falls"

Also from
THE AUTHOR

The Dream Doctor Mysteries

Dream Student

Dream Doctor

Dream Child

Dream Family

Waking Dream

Dream Reunion

Dream Home

Dream Vacation

Fever Dream

Dream Wedding

Dream Fragments: Stories from the Dream Doctor Mysteries

Betty & Howard's Excellent Adventure

A Box of Dreams: the collected

Dream Doctor Mysteries (books 1-5)

Dream Sequence (the Dream Doctor Mysteries, books 1-3)

The Jane Barnaby Adventures

Finders Keepers

Losers Weepers

Her Brother's Keeper

The Jane Barnaby Adventures Box Set

Mr. Smith and the Roach

Welcome to Romance
Finding Dori
A Reel Christmas in Romance

Blessings of Love
Twice Blessed

All books available in paperback, and as Audible audiobooks!

All available at:
www.amazon.com
and
www.jjdibenedetto.com

Author's
NOTE

$\mathcal{I}$f you've read some of my other books, you'll probably recognize a few characters and locations in this book that have shown up elsewhere. That's particularly true of the main characters, Jon and Sheryl. They're supporting characters in the third book of the Jane Barnaby Adventures, Her Brother's Keeper, but I really felt like they deserved a starring role, and I finally got around to giving it to them.

If you happened to watch General Hospital back in the 1990's, Jon and Sheryl might be familiar to you for another reason – they were inspired by my favorite couple on the show (still my favorite TV couple ever), Kevin and Lucy, brought memorably to life by Jon Lindstrom and Lynn Herring. So this book is a little bit of a love letter to them.

I hope you enjoyed this book, and if you did, you haven't seen the last of Jon and Sheryl and all their friends (and enemies!). To keep up with my latest developments and all the news on new books, you can visit my website at www. jjdibenedetto.com, or my Facebook fan page at

www.facebook.com/JJDiBenedettoAuthor

About the
AUTHOR

J.J. (James) DiBenedetto is a marketing professional by day and novelist by night. He lives in lovely Arlington, Virginia with his beautiful wife and a very demanding cat who runs the house. He's the author of the Dream Doctor Mysteries, the Jane Barnaby Adventures, Mr. Smith and the Roach and other works.

About the
COVER ARTIST

Rossano Designs is a small company run by an independently published author to support other authors. Rachel Rossano enjoys designing. Rossano Designs is her way of helping others give their stories professional covers and presentation at a reasonable price.

WWW.FACEBOOK.COM/ROSSANODESIGNS/

About the
BOOK DESIGNER

Ever since childhood, Colleen has been obsessed with how words flow across a page. It's only natural that she design and typeset book interiors to help keep independent publishers professional and tens of thousands of words easy on the readers' eyes.

WWW.AMPERSANDBOOKINTERIORS.COM

Made in the USA
Middletown, DE
24 December 2020

26715339R00135